Naughty

BEDTIME STORIES

Naughty

BEDTIME STORIES

Joan Elizabeth Lloyd

HEAT
NEW YORK, NEW YORK

THE BERKLEY PUBLISHING GROUP
Published by the Penguin Group
Penguin Group (USA) Inc.
375 Hudson Street, New York, New York 10014, USA
Penguin Group (Canada), 10 Alcorn Avenue, Toronto, Ontario M4V 3B2, Canada
(a division of Pearson Penguin Canada Inc.)
Penguin Books Ltd., 80 Strand, London WC2R 0RL, England
Penguin Group Ireland, 25 St. Stephen's Green, Dublin 2, Ireland (a division of Penguin Books Ltd.)
Penguin Group (Australia), 250 Camberwell Road, Camberwell, Victoria 3124, Australia
(a division of Pearson Australia Group Pty. Ltd.)
Penguin Books India Pvt. Ltd., 11 Community Centre, Panchsheel Park, New Delhi - 110 017, India
Penguin Group (NZ), Cnr. Airborne and Rosedale Roads, Albany, Auckland 1310, New Zealand
(a division of Pearson New Zealand Ltd.)
Penguin Books (South Africa) (Pty.) Ltd., 24 Sturdee Avenue, Rosebank, Johannesburg 2196, South Africa

Penguin Books Ltd., Registered Offices: 80 Strand, London WC2R 0RL, England

NAUGHTY BEDTIME STORIES

A Heat book / published by arrangement with Bookspan
Copyright © 2003 by Joan Elizabeth Lloyd.
Text design by Stacy Irwin.

PRINTING HISTORY
Venus Book Club hardcover edition / 2003
HEAT trade paperback edition / May 2005

This book has been catalogued with the Library of Congress.

ISBN: 0-425-20246-1

PRINTED IN THE UNITED STATES OF AMERICA

10 9 8 7 6 5 4 3 2 1

Contents

Introduction

Dear Reader,

I've been writing erotic stories professionally for almost fifteen years, and for my own enjoyment for lots of years before that. One thing I've learned is that, of all the literary forms, the erotic story is the most individual. There's something very personal about erotica, and a given story either hits just the right spot or it misses badly. One person's turn-on is another's turnoff.

Therefore I've included stories of many types. There's the straightforward encounter tale: meet, do it, then end everything, like "Sleigh Ride" or "At a Bar"; the slightly unconventional, like "Tunnel of Love" or "Couch Potato"; and the really off center, like "In My Dreams" or the two parts of "The Incredible Orgasm Machine." I've included some science fiction stories about a fictional world where sex is open and creative, and two featuring erotic deamons who visit in the night—or do they?

—J.E.L.

To My Phantom Lover

To my phantom lover,

I've lived our evening together in my mind so many times I know exactly how it's going to be.

You arrive. I'm dressed in a long skirt and soft silky blouse. I wear nothing beneath so I can feel my clothing as it whispers over my body. Soon it will be your hands, your mouth. But not yet. First, I remove your coat and warm your cold hands against my cheeks. I hold your palms and look deeply into your eyes, my gaze telling you all the things I can never tell you to your face, my love. I slide my hands to your wrists, then along your cloth-covered forearms to your shoulders. I frame your face, then slip my fingers into your soft hair, caressing your scalp. My lips come ever closer to yours until we're merely a breath apart.

Oh, lover, I savor the anticipation and feel myself moisten and swell. Finally, without a word, we kiss. The kiss is soft at first, lips brushing lips, tongues lightly touching, then we pull each other closer, deepening the kiss until we are enmeshed, part of one another. Your breath is mine and mine yours. Your tongue strokes, delves, explores, and begs mine to do the same. I sample the softness of the warm depths of your mouth, the hard smooth surface of your teeth, the rough texture of your insinuating tongue.

You pull back enough to nip my lower lip, biting just hard enough to create shards of pleasure that knife through my body, making my nipples tighten and my breasts swell, reaching for your touch. You take the lead, now threading your fingers through my hair, nibbling, placing love bites along the line of my jaw, then sucking on the lobe of my ear.

My knees are weak now but I won't rush any of our time together. I let my head fall back, revealing my throat for your mouth to pleasure. You know just what I love, tiny licks and kisses along the taut tendon at the side of my neck, then to the incredibly sensitive spot where it meets my shoulder. Heat! Heat flows through me like hot lava, turning my bones to melting wax. God, how I want you. Don't rush but hurry! I want it all. I want to give you all!

Your breath is hot in my ear now as you guide me to the

bed. Before I'm too weak to stand you unbutton my skirt and use your palms to guide it down over my hips and thighs. Where the cloth slithers down my skin your hands follow blazing paths of fire. Now I am naked from the waist down, yet my blouse is still buttoned across my aching breasts. You laugh softly, enjoying the sight of me, half prim and half wanton. I raise my hands to unfasten my blouse but you push them away. Not yet.

I stand beside the bed, my knees almost buckling while you undress. I try to help, but you know my shaking hands would only get in your way. Efficiently you remove your clothing until I can see you in your magnificent nakedness. You are so beautiful and I let my eyes roam over your body. Wide shoulders, lightly furred chest, muscular thighs. And your penis is hard, fully erect, stretching toward me, your full testicles hanging beneath. As I look I can almost feel you slowly penetrating, opening me, filling me, and I can feel fluid dribbling down the inside of my thighs.

Now you hold me close, rubbing your chest against mine with the silky layer of fabric between. The sensation is electric, silk sliding over my tight nipples, your hands pressing me ever more tightly against you. I undulate, moving against you like a cat in heat, pressing my naked mound against your rampant erection. Your hands move down my back to my naked buttocks to press your penis more firmly against my flesh, so close but not yet penetrating. There is no space between us, skin to skin, except for the silk. I want it gone. I want my bare breasts against your chest, my nipples almost tangled in your chest hair. As I try to remove it, however, you stop me. Your eyes tell me how sensual it feels, how wicked to see me half dressed when you're so naked, so I drop my hands.

You lower me to the bed and I stretch out on the cool linen sheets, feeling the slightly rough material against my calves. I rub the soles of my feet against the linen, then against your hard thighs. I touch your hardness with my toes while you stand beside the bed. I watch your penis harden still more, jumping as I press it against your belly with the sole of my foot.

Unable to stand more teasing, you growl, then lower yourself beside me. Your mouth finds my nipple and you wet my blouse with your lips and tongue. As you move from side to side, the moisture is cool on one breast, hot with your breath on the other. Your teeth find my hard nub and your erotic bites cause my back to arch against you. I want more but you give me only bits, hints of the wildness to come. And it will be wild. This is only the calm before the storm.

Suddenly your hand finds my mound, your fingers combing through my pussy hair, pressing places filled with heat and need. You laugh again when you feel how wet I am, knowing I am also a reflection of your hardness. Find me, I cry silently. Find all the places that need your hands, your body. Now! Find me!

Yet you still play, teasing me, sliding through the wetness, exploring all the creases, not touching where I need you. Well, two can play this game. I find your cock with my hand and encircle it. Slowly and softly I slide up and down its length, not squeezing the way I know you want me to. As long as you keep teasing me, I'll keep teasing you. If I can keep from losing my mind.

With only a shred of conscious thought left, I cup your testicles, weighing them in my palm. So hot—so hungry. Now! I scream soundlessly. Please! Your fingers find my clitoris and I almost explode. I reach for nirvana, yet it eludes me. Please, just rub a moment more. One more stroke. Please!

You move and when your mouth finds my clit, I shatter, my climax echoing through my entire being. I squeeze your cock, driving it through my fingers in a parody of thrusting. More! Spasms continue to riot through me and you move to position your cock between my spread thighs. Now! Do it! You insert the tip just a bit but it's not enough. Not enough! I wrap my legs around your waist and impale myself on your shaft, taking all of you deeply, completely.

Your moans and growls match mine, sounds of intensity, of need, of power and glorious erotic electricity. Higher and higher we ride the wave, my body still coming, squeezing your cock imbedded within me. With a shout you shudder and I feel each pulse of your cock, your buttocks, your balls.

Finally we are spent. We stay joined and slip into sleep.

• • •

Marcy had written her letter the previous evening, sealed it in a white velum envelope and addressed it to "My Phantom Lover." Now she slipped it into the pocket of her jeans as she walked down the stairs, holding her seven-month-old baby. As usual, her husband Joe sat at the breakfast table, reading his newspaper and sipping coffee poured from the timed pot they had put up the night before.

"Good morning, precious," Joe said to his baby daughter, rising to kiss the top of her head.

"Ga," the baby said as Marcy surrendered her daughter to the arms of her husband. Silently she moved around the table and slipped the envelope into Joe's business case. He'd find it later, she knew, and he'd know. By the time he arrived home the baby would be at her mother's house, ready to stay for the night, and they'd have the entire evening together. Marcy sighed. Anticipation was almost as wonderful as what would come later.

She smiled.

Read Aloud

"What are you reading?" Joe asked his wife.

Eve jumped at the sound of his voice, so deeply involved in her book she obviously hadn't heard him come into the bedroom. She glanced at the clock. "Wow, it's late. Are you done with your work?"

"Finally. It took me almost four hours to get those projections ready for the meeting tomorrow. I hate having to bring work home."

"Me too, but it happens so rarely that it's not a real problem. You look beat," Eve said, hiding the cover of her book with her hand. "Are you too jazzed up to sleep?"

"I certainly hope not. I've got to be fresh for Norm and the clients at nine sharp."

"Well," Eve said, putting the book on the floor out of Joe's sight, still open to the page she was reading, "why don't you get ready for bed and I'll put on the news. I might read a bit more."

As she reached for the TV remote, her husband asked again, "I wondered what you were reading. You looked so intent when I came in. I stood there for several minutes and you didn't even notice I was in the room."

Eve reached down, eased the book shut, and quickly slid it under the bed. "It's nothing special. Just a sappy romance novel."

Joe circled the room and looked down at his wife. "You're embarrassed. I've never seen you like this." He gazed at the side of the bed. "We don't usually have secrets."

"Okay," Eve said as she groped and found the book. She held it up and Joe looked at the cover he had seen when he entered the room. It was black with the face of an attractive, well-made-up woman. "Erotic Tales for Women," he read. "Romance novel?"

"Well, maybe it's a bit more than that. It intrigued me so I got it from the book club. It's really hot."

"Hot how?"

"It's stories of really explicit sex. You know, the kind of stuff they have in those novels set in Hollywood about what stars do with each other."

"You looked like you were really enjoying the story you were reading. Read a bit to me."

Eve was horrified. There was no way she could read any of the salacious material out loud. She held out the book. "You read whatever you want."

Joe took the book, glanced at the page, then handed it back. He sat down on the edge of the bed and said, "It looks good. Read me some."

Eve swallowed hard. "I couldn't. It's too, too . . ."

"It might make it easier for me to sleep if you read aloud."

Eve's laugh was nervous. "Not a chance. It's not at all relaxing."

"Maybe not for you, but it would amuse me. Please?"

Eve loved her husband of four years, and she would do almost anything he asked. Almost.

"Please," he said, cocking his head to one side. A lock of hair fell across his forehead and he put on a boyish smile. "Please, mommy, read to me."

Eve laughed. He knew she couldn't resist him when he looked at her like that. She flipped to the beginning of the story she had just read. "This one's about a genie who grants the hero one wish. He wishes that his lover would let him do, and want him to do, exactly what he wants. A silly premise, but it leads to some great sex." She swallowed again.

"Does it start with the sexy stuff?" Joe asked.

"Not right away. There has to be some story first."

"I want to hear the sexy parts, so cut to the good stuff."

"His name is Hakim and she's Ermine." Eve flipped a few pages. "He goes into her room and she's in bed, asleep."

"Umm. Sounds good so far."

Eve found her place and started to read. "Hakim sat on the edge of the bed and gently awakened Ermine with sensual kisses on her neck and face. She opened her eyes and stared at him. 'Good evening, Hakim,' she said. 'What brings you into my chamber so late?'

" 'I wanted to see you,' he said, 'and kiss you.' "

Joe put his hand on the book. "Skip the pleasantries and the kissing."

Eve looked at the gleam in his eye. "Right. No pleasantries." She turned another page. "The kiss ended and he pulled the silken sheet down to reveal her body, clad only in a sheer nightdress. She was so beautiful, her breasts firm, her nipples deep brown. 'I want to touch you,' he asked, hoping the genie had indeed granted his wish.

" 'Oh, yes, please. Touch me,' Ermine said softly, quickly removing her nightdress.

" 'Where may I touch you?' Hakim asked. 'Tell me.' There was a long pause, then Ermine whispered, 'Anywhere you like.' "

Joe pulled down the blanket covering his wife. She was dressed in a pair of satin pajamas. As Eve gazed into her husband's eyes, he stroked his hands over her breasts, then pulled one silk-covered button at a time out through its buttonhole.

He parted the cloth of the pajama top and Eve felt cool air caress her skin as heat gathered in her breasts.

"Your nipples are already erect," Joe said. "May I touch them?"

She let out a long breath. "Yes."

"Good. But you have to keep reading."

She took in another deep breath. "This is really difficult," she said, feeling his fingers swirl over the white skin of her breasts.

"I know. It turns me on." His eyes raked over her naked body. "Read."

"Hakim took a nipple in his fingers and rolled it until it became tight and hard." Eve felt her husband do exactly what Hakim was doing in the story. She felt the heat build in her belly. "Then Ermine felt his hands move lower, his fingertips stroking the naked flesh of her belly." It was getting harder to breathe with Joe's fingers caressing her.

"Ermine parted her thighs and Hakim smiled. The genie's promise was coming true." Without thinking, Eve lifted her hips so Joe could pull her pajama pants off. Then she spread her legs and cleared her throat. "Hakim's fingers played with the wiry hair between Ermine's thighs, gently pulling, making her feel what was happening, testing the genie's power. Ermine merely smiled, then closed her eyes."

When Eve closed her eyes, Joe said, "You can't read with your eyes closed. Keep going."

Eve had reached the place where she had stopped reading, so the rest of the story was new to her. "Slowly Hakim's fingers pushed until they were delving into the secret folds of her . . ."

"Her what?" Joe asked.

Eve cleared her throat. "Her body."

Joe grabbed the book and read the section. He handed the book back to his wife. "That's not what it says."

"I know, but I can't say those words."

Joe's fingers slid through Eve's wet folds, skimming the sides of her erect clit. "Yes, you can. I won't go any farther until you read exactly what's in that book. It says 'secret folds of her pussy'. So you must say it just that way."

Eve's body was on fire. Joe knew exactly what and where to touch to make her body hungry for him and he touched every tiny square of skin she liked. He blew a stream of cool air on her hot flesh, then stopped stroking her, leaving his fingers immobile so she could feel his heat. "Read," he said.

Taking a deep breath, Eve focused her eyes on the offending words. "Delving into the secret folds of her . . ." Her voice dropped. ". . . pussy."

"Good girl," Joe said, resuming his ministrations. "Okay. Keep reading. What does he do next?"

Her voice slightly hoarse, Eve continued. "Hakim's fingers were everywhere, rubbing and stroking, until Ermine felt she was going to explode. Then, slowly, he inserted one finger into her . . ." Eve looked up, then said, ". . . pussy."

Joe's finger entered her and she thought she would come right then. "'Does that feel good?' Hakim asked. 'Oh yes,' Ermine answered. 'It makes me want more.' Hakim was delighted, and soon a second, then a third finger joined the first."

Eve's pussy was filled with Joe's fingers, gently thrusting and withdrawing. "Read ahead. Do they fuck?"

Eve's eyes raced over the page. "Yes," she said. "They do."

"Do what?"

"They make love. Here at the bottom of the page."

Fingers still moving in his wife's cunt, Joe said, "I didn't ask whether they made love. I wanted to know whether they fucked."

"They do."

"Do what? Say it."

He wants me to say that word. Eve had never used such language, but reading the explicit phrases always made her tremble. She took another deep breath. "They fuck."

"Oh God, baby." Suddenly, Joe was out of his clothes and his cock replaced his fingers inside his wife. "Tell me. What are we doing?"

Eve gasped. Her body lifted to meet Joe's thrusts, her fingers gripped his naked shoulders, her nails digging into his skin. "Fucking."

"Shit," he hissed. "My cock is inside your . . . Say it."

"My pussy." She could barely control her voice.

He pistoned harder. "What's inside your pussy?"

"Your cock's inside of my pussy." Hot pleasure knifed through her body, from her breasts to her cunt. She wrapped her legs around Joe's waist and pulled him more tightly inside of her. "Fuck me. Please. Harder."

He pounded into her, the two of them crazed with the excitement of it. Together they soared, and finally Eve felt the colors burst apart, reds and blues, greens and oranges filling her head. She heard Joe groan, then felt his body tighten and his back arch. She grabbed his hard ass-cheeks and held him as tightly against her as she could as their orgasms blended and entwined.

Still wrapped in each other they collapsed on the bed, breathless and nearly unconscious.

Later, Joe moaned, "Holy shit. That was the best."

"Yes, it was." Eve grinned. "The best what?"

Joe propped himself on his elbow and looked down at his wife. "That was the best fuck ever."

Eve giggled. "Yeah, it was. Let's hear it for erotic stories."

Joe snuggled down against his wife. "And they say good sex makes a great sleeping pill." He grinned. "Of course that's why I did it."

"Right. It was just medicine. And if I believe that . . ."

How Does He Do That?

The party was in full swing when I arrived. As I dumped my coat in the pile on Greta's bed I heard loud music, lots of laughter, and raucous conversation. Noise isn't usually my style for a party but that night I needed to get away from my tiny apartment. It was the six-month anniversary of Rick's departure and I didn't want to spend the evening home, thinking about our now-defunct relationship. Time to get out and get going, I told myself as I straightened my black skirt and soft pink blouse. Time to get back into life and stop pining for the jerk.

So I emerged from the bedroom into a swirling mass of people. No, I told myself, I'm not going to think about how deafening it is, I'm not going to spoil it for myself before anything's started. I worked my way to the bar and poured myself a glass of white wine. I mingled with a few old friends but I was getting nowhere. No wonderful rich man swept me off my feet. No guy with a gorgeous body invited me to jump into his bed and forget all my troubles.

"Is that what you want?" a male voice behind me said in my ear.

I whirled around and looked into a thick pair of glasses. "Excuse me?" I said, taking in his balding head, rumpled tweed jacket, and loose-fitting jeans.

"I asked whether jumping into bed with a handsome hunk was what you wanted."

It was difficult to tell what he looked like since the thick lenses magnified his eyes until he had the look of a frightened monkey. "I didn't say a thing about jumping into bed with anyone."

"You didn't say it, but that was what you were thinking, wasn't it?"

"Don't be ridiculous."

"I'm not. And let's see." He put a hand in the middle of my back and turned me toward the mass of people. "Over there." He indicated a hunky guy who obviously lifted weights heavier than horses. "That's Tad. He's got an IQ just above that of a houseplant but he's always willing, anxious actually, to jump into bed with anyone who's breathing." The man's voice softened. "And you're certainly much more than just anyone."

"What . . . ?"

"Don't stop me. I'm on a roll." He motioned toward a tall, slender man with a huge brushy moustache. "I understand that his moustache has tickled the nipples of more women than can be counted without electronic assistance."

I tried, unsuccessfully, to suppress a smile.

"And Mike over there. He's rich, unattached, and very willing. What more can one ask?"

"Okay, okay. I get your point. But who the hell are you?"

"My name's Steven and I'm not rich." He smiled a slightly self-deprecating smile and continued, "I'm not hunky either, but I'd love to get to know you better. As a matter of fact, I'd like to get to know you as well as you'll let me. I can make your body sing."

I blinked a few times. The nerve of this guy. "You're charming but, as much as I might have thought that was what I was looking for, I've realized that I'm not going to jump into bed with anyone tonight."

"A pity. I'll bet your body is delicious, especially those wonderful wet places that taste so fantastic." It was suddenly hard to breathe. He took my hand. "I'd love to slide my tongue over a hard clit and lap up the juices that flow so freely when I suck on the hard nub. And when I slide my finger deep inside a cunt, then add another and another until it's so full and hot, well . . ."

I swallowed hard. "Thanks for the invitation," I said, my

voice barely a squeak, "but I'm really not interested." I wanted to move away, lose myself in the crowd. Get my coat and run. But my body wouldn't move from this man's side.

"I'm sorry. I didn't mean to frighten you. It's just that you bring out all the worst thoughts in me. I saw you looking a bit lost. I asked Greta and found out a little about you. I felt this magnetic thing between us. Don't you feel it?"

I did, but did I want to admit it? "Yes," I whispered.

"I knew it. I can feel what you're thinking, you know. Consider how great that would make us in bed."

"You've got quite a line, Steven," I said, wondering what it might be like to just let go and allow him to fuck my brains out. "But you're coming on a bit too fast for me."

"No, actually I'm not. And I'd love to fuck your brains out."

"That's the second time you've done that." He was very tempting, and a bit scary. "Do you really know what I'm thinking?"

"I know that you're thinking that I'm tempting and scary." He smiled softly and gazed at me through his thick glasses. "I really hope I'm tempting you because you're tempting me to do all kinds of delicious things to your beautiful body."

Again I swallowed hard. He looked so harmless, but my palms were sweating and my pussy was creaming and twitching.

"My apartment's one floor down and I can promise you that I'm as harmless or harmful as you want me to be."

He took my elbow and, without a word, guided me out the

door and down to his apartment. As he shut the door behind us, he said, softly, "I would offer you a drink or something, but I know that's not what you want."

What did I want? I wanted him to make all the decisions, to just do it and make me scream with pleasure.

He chuckled. "Of course." He wrapped one arm around my waist and pulled me close. He tangled his fingers in my short hair and pulled my head back so his mouth could explore my throat. It was as though he knew every special place on my body. Others had said that I had a weakness for having my neck nibbled and he seemed to know that instinctively. He pulled slightly harder on my hair and the sting on my scalp raised my excitement to a higher level.

"You taste so good," he growled. Then his fingers were opening the buttons of my blouse and his warm palm was against my bra-covered breasts. It was as though he knew exactly what I wanted and when. He pinched my nipples through the fabric and when I thought I couldn't stand it anymore, he unhooked the front clasp and filled his hands with my flesh.

I couldn't think, couldn't act, couldn't do anything on my own. I could just respond to his touch, to the pressure of his obvious erection against my pubic bone. A hand slid down my spine and pressed my pelvis harder against his cock. I rubbed against his body like an animal in heat, wanting, needing, aching for his hands, his mouth, his body.

I have no idea how we got naked and ended up on his bed but almost magically we were there. His hands and then his mouth were precisely where I needed them to be, rubbing my slit, nipping at my pussy lips, sucking on my clit. He drew my clit into his mouth, then squeezed it lightly between his tight lips. One finger was inside me, then two, then three, stretching me, making me feel so much. "God," I screamed, "do it."

"You only think you want it now. You can wait."

Higher and higher he drove me, able to bring more pleasure from my body than I thought possible. I heard the familiar ripping of a foil package. Now he's going to fuck me.

"Not just yet," he said. I opened my eyes and saw that he had put the condom over his thumb. Then he resumed rubbing my cunt. Suddenly, that cold, slippery, condom-covered finger was rubbing my asshole. No one had ever touched me there before but, once over my knee-jerk withdrawal, I had to admit it pushed me closer and closer to the edge.

"I know how good that feels," he said. "I can soar with you. Share it with me."

Somehow I opened my mind and he was flying with me, part of my incredible arousal. Another foil package. "Yes, now." He rubbed his cock over my steaming cunt, cool latex against fiery flesh. Then he filled me, his thrusts meeting mine, his rhythm perfectly in tune with my body, his mind sailing through the flashing colors of my impending climax.

I wanted to make it last, but it was impossible. "I know," he said, his voice hoarse. "There will be other times. Let go. NOW!"

We came together, spasms rocking our joined bodies, harsh cries filling the night. Slowly, our minds separated.

I think I slept for a while, waking as Steven pulled a quilt over us both. We hardly know each other, I thought, yet I've had the most satisfying sex I've had in—well, in maybe ever.

"I'm glad it was satisfying, and we'll get to know each other better. We have lots of time."

"How do you do that?" I said, totally puzzled. "You seem to know what I'm thinking."

"I do know what you're thinking and, at times of great emotional upheaval, I can be with you in your mind too. I can share your orgasms and you can share mine. It multiplies the strength of each."

"But how?"

"We have a long time to share everything. For now, suffice it to say that it will be fantastic between us for a very long time."

I sighed. "It sure was fantastic, however you did it." I cuddled into his arms and fell asleep.

The Beast

Marissa lay on the pile of furs and thought about the amazing two weeks she had spent with The Beast. The Beast. She had asked his name several times and he had always refused to tell her. It's funny, she reflected, she had begun to think of him as "the beast" from the first moment she had awakened in the cave. Now it was just his name. The Beast.

She shook her head as she recalled those awful days before The Beast. She had been driven out of her home by her abusive stepfather and she had wandered through fields and woods until she was far away from her village. She had lived on berries and a stolen loaf of bread, curling up at night beneath a tree, crying herself to sleep. One morning it had begun to snow and after hours of walking she had finally collapsed, waiting to die.

When she had opened she eyes, she had been warm and dry. "Are you hungry?" a soft voice had asked.

"Oh yes," she had said, turning to see the man who had spoken. To her horror, she had seen him, The Beast. He was mostly bear, but he walked on two legs and spoke like a man. She smiled now, remembering how she had screamed, and how he had quickly soothed her.

Over the weeks that followed, he had fed her and tended to her frozen fingers and toes. They had talked for long hours about anything and everything. He knew about the world far beyond the local villages and told her stories about kingdoms and castles, strange animals with long trunks that sucked water up from rivers or long necks that allowed them to reach leaves at the tops of the tallest trees.

Most of the time he had tried to keep out of her line of sight but soon it didn't matter. She found she could ignore his appearance as he had become the best friend she had ever had. Several times she had given him a quick kiss on his furry cheek, hoping he was an enchanted prince and she could awaken him from the spell. Alas, it hadn't worked.

Now, as she lay between waking and sleeping, she knew he was turning down the lamps in the cave, preparing to bed down in his corner. "Can we talk for a few minutes?" she asked, gazing at the single candle still burning beside her pallet.

"Of course," The Beast said. "What would you like to talk about?"

"I don't know. I feel restless and warm all over. I feel secret things in secret places." She could hear him snuffling around, huffing and clearing his throat.

"Those are probably secret woman things," he said softly, "about which I could know nothing. You could tell me about it if you like but I'm afraid . . ."

"There was a boy in my village. He was tall and handsome and all the girls used to giggle and talk about how virile he must be. They would talk about what they would do if they could be alone with him in the woods. They never talked to me, of course, but I listened and it made me feel like I do now."

"Oh," The Beast said. "How's that?"

"I feel tingly here," she said, rubbing her palms over her breasts. "And soft and bubbly low in my belly. My stepfather used to accuse me of being a tease, tormenting him with thoughts of coupling. But I'm not teasing, it's just the way I feel."

"Did he ever . . . ?"

"No. Certainly not. He's old and ugly." She could hear The Beast's quick intake of breath. "Oh, I'm sorry. He's not at all like you. You're not old and you're not ugly at all. I think you're wonderful."

"I know that I'm like a brother to you," The Beast said with a sigh. He paused, then continued, "I do so wish I could be more." She could hear him shrug.

She thought about his furry body, his handlike paws, and sighed. "I wish you could be too, because you're the best friend I've ever had. What would you do if you could?"

"Oh Marissa. If I could, I would make love to you."

"How?"

She heard another long, drawn-out sigh. "If I had lips instead of a snout I would kiss you. I would feel your lips on mine, taste your mouth, nibble on your lips."

Marissa rubbed her fingers over her mouth, almost feeling The Beast's lips.

"I would hold you close, feel your skin."

She wanted him as a woman wants a man, yet he was The Beast. She felt her body heat and knew that she had to have something. Marissa pulled off her blouse and ran her hands over her flesh. "Would you touch my breasts?"

"You have such beautiful breasts. I dream about them at night, wishing, hoping I could become a man, just for a few moments, so I could hold them and lick them."

Marissa stroked her breasts, pulling at her hardened nipples. He wouldn't come to her so she picked up the stubby candle and moved it beside his bed of blankets so he could look at her. She knelt beside him, lifted her breasts and said, "Touch me."

He lifted his pawlike hands. "Not with these. You should be touched by a man with soft skin and long fingers."

"I will close my eyes and imagine, if you like." She lowered her eyelids. She felt the soft brush of fur against her heated skin and joined it with the stroking of her own hands. "Yes," she sighed, her hands gliding lower.

She allowed her head to drop back as her fingers reached the nest of her hair. "Put your hands on mine," she said. "That way you can feel what I feel."

When she felt his hesitation, she whispered, "Please. Share this with me."

He placed the backs of his hands/paws over hers lightly as she stroked herself. "Yes. I can share this with you this way." Marissa was no stranger to pleasuring herself so she knew exactly where to touch. She rubbed gently over her clit, feeling the soft fur of The Beast's hands over hers. "Tell me, can you feel it?"

"Oh, yes," The Beast said. "This is more than I ever dreamed I could have."

"Let me show you even more." She took his hand and placed the soft pads over her wetness. She felt him hold his long claws away from her body.

"No," he groaned, "I'll hurt you."

"You couldn't." She put her hands over his and pressed, moving her hips so the pressures were just right. "Just like that," she moaned. "Don't move!"

She wiggled her hips and tightened her thighs until she felt the spasms of climax boiling through her body. "Don't move!" she cried again.

Suddenly she felt fingers, not claws, fingers dipping into her, urging more from her already spasming body. Again she climbed and again she dove over the edge. Then she felt lips against hers. Too deep into her pleasure to wonder what was happening, she wrapped her arms around an all-too-male body. "Do it," she cried and his hard cock drove into her, yet another climax crashing over her as he thrust.

With a scream, The Beast came inside her. The candle guttered and they slept.

Hours later, Marissa awoke, and felt human arms around her. Sensing he was awake, she said, "I don't understand."

"I couldn't tell you, but there was a spell. I know it's cliché but a witch decided that unless I could entice a woman into having sex with me I was doomed to remain a beast. I had no idea how 'having sex' could work—with a beast I mean—but you made it happen."

"Are you a handsome prince?"

"Yup. Terrific looking, fabulously sexy body, jewels, and a castle. We'll be so good together. I'm really dynamite in bed— in my human form, I mean. It'll be terrific."

"Hmm. That's nice." As she fell back to sleep, Marissa wondered whether she liked him better as a beast.

Whorehouse Shoes

Whorehouse shoes. that's what I call them, and they've changed my sex life dramatically. But let me begin at the beginning.

I love garage sales and frequently, on Saturday mornings, I leave Brad with the kids and I wander. It's peaceful, fun, and sometimes life changing. One Saturday I stopped at a house with a lawn full of goodies and just rummaged through boxes of mostly old clothing. ANYTHING IN HERE FOR $1, the sign said. At the bottom of the box I found a pair of red patent-leather shoes with four-inch spike heels. Ideas ran through my mind and I couldn't suppress a smile.

I groped around and found a strapless Lurex top, black with

silver threads, and a black leather miniskirt. I found tags on each and they were both size fourteen, my size. Fate must be speaking to me, I thought, so I paid my three dollars and carefully put my purchases on the front seat of my car. Brad and I had plans to go to my sister's for dinner so I quickly called her from my cell phone and cancelled. When I got home, I didn't tell my husband.

The rest of the day was as hectic as always but I managed to make a few phone calls. Finally, at six, while I fed the kids, Brad picked up the babysitter. By six fifteen, we were off. "Make a right at the next corner," I told Brad.

"But your sister's . . ."

"Just do it," I told him. "I have a surprise for you."

"We aren't going to your sister's?" he said, a gleam in his eye.

"Nope and the rest is none of your business." Brad is used to my devious mind so he played along. I gave him directions to turn right or left at particular corners and eventually we ended up at a very fancy hotel several miles from home. "Wait in the car for fifteen minutes, then knock on the door to room 227." I had gotten the room number from a desk clerk I'd done business with before, and he had promised to leave the key beneath a potted plant at the end of the hall. As you might have gathered, I've played games at this hotel with Brad before.

I found the key and entered the room. A table set for two

stood in the corner with a meal from the hotel's restaurant warming in ovens beneath the table. I dashed into the bathroom with a small case I'd brought from home and yanked off my jeans and sweater. I pulled the black Lurex top over my bare skin and arranged my small breasts beneath the fabric. Next I slipped on black stockings with lacy stay-up tops, the black miniskirt, and finally the shoes. I held out one foot and admired the bright red vamps, ankle straps, and tall stiletto heels. Yes, I said to myself, those do the trick. Trick. I smiled at my own humor.

I added clunky silver earrings, a thick silver collar, and bangle bracelets, then fluffed my hair and darkened my makeup. As I finished I heard a knock. Brad. As I walked from the bathroom, slightly rocky on the unfamiliar heels, I found my hips swaying and my breasts bouncing. I lowered the pitch of my voice. "Just a moment."

I opened the door and watched Brad's expression change. His eyes darkened and became smoky with desire. "Well, good evening."

"Hiya, sugar," I said, affecting a southern accent. "Ya'll come on in."

"I hadn't expected such a welcome," Brad said as he closed the door behind him.

"You should have, sugar," I said. "You're quite a hunk." Brad's 5'8", a bit paunchy with a handsome face slightly hidden behind coke-bottle glasses. You might not think him a hunk, but when we're hot, we're both gorgeous. Even me with my boyish shape and stick-straight, mousy-brown hair. Who cares when I've got my whorehouse shoes on?

"You're not bad yourself," he said, his eyes roaming over my outfit. "I love your clothes," he continued, "especially your shoes."

"Like them?" I asked, holding out my leg so we could admire the shoes.

"Oh yes," Brad said. "I like the whole look."

I reached behind me and used my hands to boost myself onto the dresser until I was sitting, knees wide, with my back to the mirror. "How much do you like it?"

He quickly pulled his sweatshirt off over his head, then knelt on the floor between my legs. One hand on each knee, he pulled my legs still farther apart and dove into my pussy. When Brad's really hot, he's in no mood for preliminaries. I like that in a guy. Let me tell you I was already soaking wet, likewise in no mood for foreplay.

His mouth found my pussy while he dragged my top down to my waist. Fingers pulled at my nipples as his mouth went to work on my clit. I couldn't concentrate on either action. Both his hands and his mouth were driving me crazy. Tongue probed, fingers pinched, tongue licked long strokes, fingers swirled, tongue stabbed, fingers rolled my nipples until I almost cried out. Then I exploded, wave upon wave of orgasm crashing over me. As I started to come down, he pushed me higher again.

I must have come three or four times before he lifted me off the dresser and guided me to the bed. We had occupied this room before and knew the mirror could be positioned to reflect the goings-on on the bed, so Brad quickly spread me wide and showed me my image. "Look at my slut," he said. "Hair wild, makeup smeared, legs spread to receive my cock."

My reflection was exactly as he had said, a wanton, silver top and miniskirt bunched around my waist, stockings outlining my pussy, whorehouse shoes propping my knees up. I gazed at myself while Brad quickly removed his clothes. Then he stood beside the bed, eyes flicking from me to his hands massaging his hard cock. "You're a tease, taking all I give and giving me nothing." It was a familiar line that we'd used in play before.

"I'll give you more than you can handle," I growled, "if you get over here."

"Not just yet," he said, stroking his erection. "You just watch and think about what it will be like when I ram it into you."

I watched. His hands played with his cock, then stroked his balls. He took some of the sticky fluid that leaked from the tip of his cock and rubbed it around his shaft. "Want it, slut?"

"Oh yes," I groaned, wanting him despite my previous orgasms. I slipped my fingers between my legs and pushed two into my sopping pussy. "Right here," I said. I stroked my clit with my other hand and turned my eyes to the mirror. I was quite a sight, hands working. I looked back at Brad's cock. "Right here, right now."

"Right now," he said, climbing onto the bed and positioning himself between my legs. He crouched over me without touching me, then slowly entered me. The feel of his cock, the only part of his body I could feel, slowly opening me, was heaven. "Like that, slut?"

"God, yes," I said. "Do it more, do it more."

"Beg," he growled.

"Please, please." This was another old game, guaranteed to excite us still further.

"Please what?"

I knew what he wanted to hear, but I wanted to stretch it out. "Please."

Slowly he pulled his cock out until only the tip remained inside me. "Please what," he demanded.

"Please—" I paused, "—please fuck me."

With those words, he rammed into me full length. With just a few thrusts we both came, trying not to scream loud enough to disturb any neighbors.

Brad collapsed on top of me. "I love it that this room is at the end of the hall," he said, panting. "That way there are fewer people who can hear us yell and call the cops."

I laughed. "I love this room because we've done so many outrageous things here."

"I love you," Brad said. "And I must admit that I loved this evening. Where did you get those wonderful shoes?"

"My whorehouse shoes? I found them at a garage sale this morning. Can you imagine anyone getting rid of them?" I held up my foot and twisted my ankle this way and that.

"Not a chance. You're keeping them."

"You bet."

Succubus

Succubus: *noun—a female demon supposed to descend upon and have sexual intercourse with a man while he sleeps.*

Toby sat with the dictionary on his lap. They were real, or at least the word was real. He'd been watching a program about witches and demons on TV and they'd shown a picture of a gorgeous woman with wings, crouched on the footboard of a bed. God, he'd love to have one of them slip into his room while he was sleeping. He closed his eyes and tried to envision a scantily clothed voluptuous she-demon mounting his stiff cock while he slept, except he wouldn't be sleeping. Not a chance.

As the image became clearer his cock got harder. "Stop it,"

he told himself. "At this rate you'll never get to sleep. He slammed the dictionary and made his way to the bedroom. It was after eleven and he had to be at work at eight the following morning. He stripped and, wearing only a pair of cotton briefs, slid between the sheets and curled on his side. "Succubus." Surprisingly, he fell asleep quickly.

His eyes flew open. Something was in the room with him. Without moving, heart pounding, he looked at the clock. Two fifty-one. He heard the rustling sound again, a sound so soft that it wouldn't have awakened any sound sleeper. Toby, however, had always slept very lightly. With a great effort, he kept his breathing even and turned on his back as though just moving in his sleep. He opened his eyes a tiniest crack and, through his lashes, he looked toward the foot of the bed.

The room was relatively bright, with what must have been full moonlight shining in around his blinds, outlining a shape standing at the foot of his bed. "I know you're not asleep," a soft, melodious female voice said.

He slowly opened his eyes the rest of the way. She wasn't as he had pictured her at all. Rather than dark and evil-looking, she was blonde, her hair in soft waves falling over her chest, covering her naked breasts. Naked? He had pictured her dressed in some kind of filmy garment, but this woman was totally nude. From what he could see, she had long, shapely legs, full hips, and a narrow waist. Her hair covered most of the front of her body as he tried to make out her nipples and the area at the apex of her thighs.

"Do you want to see all of me?" she asked. When he remained too stunned to speak, she slowly finger-combed her hair behind her shoulders. He just stared. While he couldn't make out the details, he could see that her breasts were full, with darker centers, and she definitely was a natural blonde.

"I would turn on the lights for you, but even the dimmest illumination hurts my eyes. I'm sure you understand."

Understand? He had no clue what the hell was going on. A dream. This must be a dream brought on by that silly TV program. What the hell, Toby thought. I'll play along. "That's okay. What did you want?"

"You."

"Since this is a dream, and a hell of a one at that, you've got me."

"I love it when a man makes it easy for me." She pulled the sheet down to Toby's waist and stroked her long cool fingers over his hot skin. "I'll make it easy for you, too."

Easy? His cock was harder than he could ever remember and he wanted to grab her, throw her down, and ram it into her. When he tried to shift position, however, he couldn't move.

"I guess I didn't tell you that part," she said, her voice low and throaty. "I get to do everything. You do nothing."

"But . . ."

"Don't argue," she said, a smile in her voice. "It's pointless." She reached down and, through the bedclothes, squeezed his cock. "You'll get yours in due time. This is for me though. I get mine first."

Still standing beside the bed, the woman slowly slid her palms up her sides and cupped her full breasts. "I love it when a man sucks me." She leaned over, her tits hanging just out of reach of Toby's mouth. "Want to?"

"God, yes," he said, as she lowered one large, turgid nipple so it brushed his lips. He tried to raise his head but he was unable to move. The nipple rubbed back and forth over his mouth until he thought he'd come just from that.

"Don't worry," she said, "you won't come until I'm ready." Toby felt something tighten around the base of his cock, preventing the ejaculation that had seemed so close just a moment before.

Slowly, the nipple filled his mouth and he sucked. God, the fulfillment from just sucking was tremendous, but it was combined with incredible excitement. How he could be both content to suck and violently horny was a question he wasn't able to answer.

With a popping sound, the woman pulled her nipple from his mouth and replaced it with her other one. For long minutes Toby suckled, first one breast, then the other. When she finally stood up, he was both drained and aroused. "I think I'm ready for you now," she said, pulling back the covers, climbing onto the bed and straddling him. "These are in the way," she said, waving her hand over his briefs as they disappeared. How had she done that? Oh well, Toby thought, anything can happen in a dream, especially a wet dream this vivid.

His cock stuck straight up as she positioned her opening over him and slowly lowered herself onto his erection. Slowly the feeling of tightness around the base of his cock lessened as she levered her body up and down on his cock. Still unable to move, he just took what she gave, first watching her breasts bounce, then closing his eyes to savor the sensations.

Soon it became impossible not to come, and he did, bucking his hips against her sopping body, still unable to move his arms or legs. He opened his eyes to find her fingers pulling at her nipples, her head thrown back, a long moan issuing from her mouth.

For a long while she just sat on him as his cock softened, then hardened again. It only took a few moments until he felt the tightening of her vaginal muscles and he came again. It seemed he was able to climax almost constantly and for almost an hour they continued their enjoyment.

Finally she raised herself from him and again stood beside the bed. "That was wonderful," she purred. "Better than most, but then most men don't wake up. I think I like it this way best." In the semidarkness, she leaned over and placed a soft kiss on Toby's lips, then placed a hand over his eyes.

It was fully light when Toby awoke the following morning.

Glancing at the clock he saw that it was almost nine o'clock and he'd missed his morning meeting. He grabbed the phone and called his office mate, telling her that he'd been up all night with food poisoning and he'd be into the office by noon. Then he lay in bed, reliving his wonderful, incredibly realistic dream. He realized that his body was a bit sore and his cock was slightly red. Had he been masturbating in the middle of the night?

As he rose to take a shower, he noticed that his briefs were gone. He must have removed them in his sleep, right? He never found them.

Incubus

"A succubus? You've got to be kidding," Diana said to her office mate Toby. It was mid-afternoon and he'd finally told her that his story about food poisoning was a lie. "You sure do have the most amazing dreams." At first Diana had violently objected to Toby telling her his erotic dreams but over the past eight months of sort-of rooming together Diana had grown to like the ingenuous, curly-haired account executive. Although he was only in his late twenties, he already had a client base that most senior executives envied.

"I know it was a dream, Diana," he said, "but it seemed so real."

"Like the last one about the Irish girl, or the one about Jennifer Aniston."

"This one was much more realistic than any of those, and," he said, lowering his voice still more, "I can't find my underwear."

He seemed so sincere. "The briefs she magically caused to disappear?"

"Yeah. They're nowhere to be found. I can't wait to go to sleep tonight and see what happens."

"Toby, listen. You. Were. Dreaming." She separated her words for emphasis. "Your underwear will reappear at the bottom of your laundry basket and it will turn out that you had one hell of a wet dream. There are no such things as female demons who make love to men in their sleep."

"There's a male demon too, you know. I looked it up on the Net before I came in today. It's called an incubus."

"An incubus?" Diana said, picturing the male equivalent of the woman Toby had described.

"A male demon who has intercourse with women while they sleep."

Her face in a sardonic grin, Diana said, "I should be so lucky."

His face wreathed in smiles, Toby said, "Yes, you should."

That evening, Diana climbed into bed, still laughing inwardly at Toby's gullibility. Demons indeed. How ridiculous could one get? She slid her nightgowned body into bed, flipped off the light, and fell asleep quickly.

She awoke to the feeling of hands on her breasts and tried to open her eyes, then her mouth to scream. Her eyes wouldn't open. Her mouth wouldn't move, nor would her arms or legs. "I can tell you're awake," a man's voice said. She could feel the heat of his breath as he purred beside her left ear and she was simultaneously terrified and aroused. "It's all right. I'm only here for a little while, then you'll go back to sleep and believe I was a dream."

Fingers pinched her nipples lightly and pulled at them gently, causing a prickling between her legs. Was she being raped? What was holding her, making her unable to move? She thought about Toby's story and scoffed mentally. She wasn't that easy to fool and this was some sort of criminal act.

"I'm no criminal. I'm merely giving you pleasure before I take pleasure myself," the voice said. "Please don't be afraid or angry. I won't hurt you or make you sad, I promise." Suddenly, her mind accepted. His doing? It wasn't terrible. It wasn't a violation. It was such overwhelming pleasure that she immediately stopped struggling. She just felt.

"Yes, love, just relax and take the joy I can give you. I would never take without giving. I'll give you more pleasure than you've ever experienced." His mouth then covered her nipple, lightly sucking, while his fingers continued to play with her other one. "Yes, take," he said, his hot breath cooling the wet areas on her breast. "Take."

Her body was becoming fantastically aroused. Juices flowed

from her swollen pussy and she tried to spread her legs to relieve the pressure. "Of course," the voice said and her legs parted. God, she was so hungry. Now able to move slightly, she undulated, rubbing her buttocks against the sheets and alternately pressing her thighs together and parting them.

"You can't get any satisfaction that I don't give you," he growled, "and I know what you need." Fingers began to explore her flesh, sliding through the soaked folds, searching, probing, discovering every tiny spot that drove her higher. They slipped backward to the tender area between the pussy and anus, rubbing softly, then pushing against her tight ring.

"I know," he whispered. "It's supposed to be evil somehow, but it's not. It's pure pleasure. Let me show you." Determined, the finger, lubricated with her freely flowing juices, pushed against her anus and then pressed inside a tiny bit. There was pain, but her body quickly adjusted and her muscles relaxed. A small, coherent part of her brain said she should be fighting. She was being raped. Yet she wasn't. There was no terror, no shame, no feeling of violation. She felt only pure pleasure and simple acceptance.

Slowly the finger pressed more deeply into her and she flew higher and higher. Another finger caressed her clit and suddenly she came, hard and fast, muscles clenching. "Good girl. Again." And again she came, over and over, waves of almost unbearable pleasure washing over her.

"Now more," he said as he moved to cover her. Something

remained in her anus, filling her rear opening as his cock filled her pussy and his mouth again found her nipple. The stimulation was almost too much and she came again and again, unable to control the multiple orgasms that pounded her. She felt him come, then come again, a slow groan issuing from his mouth.

He collapsed on top of her and for long moments just lay there. Then he rose, passed his hand lightly over her face and whispered, "Sleep now."

She awoke the following morning refreshed. That was some dream, she thought, probably triggered by Toby's story of his encounter. Not totally unexpected. Yet as she got out of bed she realized that her nightgown was gone. Somehow she knew she'd never find it.

The Tunnel of Love

Greg was bummed. the evening at the amusement park had been great; he and his girlfriend Jill had had a wonderful time riding the roller coaster and eating cotton candy and peanuts. He had won her a couple of large stuffed animals playing knock-the-bottles-off-the-table and they had necked in the haunted house, both ending up having to button and zip quickly before exiting. He loved how she felt, how she tasted, how she purred when he touched her.

But now she had disappeared, telling him to take one last ride in the Tunnel of Love and she'd meet him later. Tunnel of Love? Alone? What a drag. As Greg scowled, he wondered whether she had something planned. His eyes lit up. It would be just like her. After all, she did know some of the folks who worked at the park. Maybe there was something cooking in that wonderfully creative brain of hers. Okay, Jill, he thought, I'll go along.

Moments later, with two life-sized stuffed dogs under his arm, he arrived at the Tunnel of Love and bought his ticket. Since it was almost closing, there were few people around and, as one in a long line of empty boats slid noisily on the track through the water toward him, he realized he'd be alone in the four-seater. Actually he'd probably be alone in the whole thing. Oh well, he said, climbing in and putting the two animals in the seat beside him, what the heck.

Several twists and turns later, he was deep in the darkened tunnel, the only illumination provided by softly colored underwater lights. Suddenly the boat jerked to a stop and all the lights went out. It was pitch black, a little spooky actually. He waggled his hand in front of his nose but he could see nothing at all. "Don't worry, it's only a temporary glitch," a disembodied voice said. "Just stay in your seat and the power will be back on soon."

What now? he wondered. The car jiggled beneath him and he felt the animals brush past his ear. Then someone sat beside him. "Jill?" he said softly. There was no answer, just a soft giggle that sounded sort of like her. "Jill, is that you?" Another soft giggle. The air was filled with perfume, the one his girlfriend had been wearing, but it could be anyone wearing her scent, couldn't it? But it had to be Jill. Right?

Without warning hands began to unbutton his shirt. He thought about saying something but then decided that this had to be a sexy game that Jill cooked up. He leaned back in the high-backed seat and let the hands have their way with him.

When the last button was open, the hands spread his shirt and slowly stroked his chest. Then a mouth skimmed over his ribs and up and down his breast bone. Jill? It had to be, didn't it? Yet this was totally unlike her. She was usually an active participant in their lovemaking, but she didn't usually initiate anything. And she certainly wasn't ever the aggressor.

A tongue licked wet paths over his chest and a mouth blew a stream of cool air over the moist trail. Long fingernails scraped over his skin. Jill didn't have long nails like that, did she? What the heck was going on here? Puzzled, he reached for the woman beside him, only to find his arms grabbed from behind. With two loud clanks, his wrists were fastened to the seat-back by what felt like handcuffs. He struggled yet couldn't work his hands free. "Jill," Greg said, "this is about enough. You know I like fun and games, but enough is enough."

There was that giggle again and the fingernails retraced their track across his chest. How had she managed all this? Greg wondered. She was beside him, yet he had been grabbed from behind. "Listen," he said, only to find a finger over his lips, stilling his protest. Then a mouth covered his. A tongue worried his lips until they parted and the kiss deepened, a tongue swirling over his teeth, playing with his tongue. Hands tangled in his hair and pulled his face more tightly against hers. He felt bare breasts press against his chest, then back off and lightly skim over his skin, naked nipples burning a path from throat to belly.

Greg wanted to reach out and grab the woman who was slowly driving him crazy but he couldn't with his hands restrained. His body, under no such restraint, had already reacted. His cock pressed against the front of his jeans making him just a bit uncomfortable.

Then hands unbuckled his belt. It was incredibly erotic, yet a bit embarrassing. He was a passive participant, not his usually active sexual self. He liked to be the one in control of sex, not someone only able to react.

"What if the lights go back on?" he asked.

Again a soft giggle as hands unzipped his fly. He felt his legs being lifted and his jeans and shorts pulled down to his knees. He was lowered then so his rear was on the painted wooden seat, his legs draped over the front of the boat. Jill couldn't have managed that alone, could she?

The seat was cold beneath his now-naked buttocks and he squirmed a bit to try to make himself a bit more comfortable. With two more loud snaps, his legs were fastened to the prow of the track-bound craft. Now he was completely helpless, legs and arms restrained, almost spread-eagled.

Hands were on his cock. He strained his eyes trying to make out who it was who so expertly manipulated his cock to its ultimate hardness, but it was no use. Now something cold was being rubbed over his cock, then more rubbing. Suddenly his cock glowed in the dark. It was totally weird, and fantastically erotic to see his cock and now his balls glowing in the otherwise total darkness. He tried to see the person who was doing all this but the illumination that the glow provided was insufficient.

The hands now glowed from the chemical goo that had been rubbed into his cock and slowly they rose to the chest of whoever it was in the seat beside him. Fingers painted swirls of the glowing material over full breasts. They were fuller than Jill's, weren't they? Maybe the nipples were bigger. The fingers made beautiful designs over the flesh and Greg longed to lick it off. The woman pinched her tits and he desperately wanted to suckle at those glowing nubs but he couldn't move. He just stared.

It seemed like hours as the woman played with her tits and the glowing cream but finally the hands returned to his aching cock. Then a mouth descended and a tongue licked the oozing fluid from the tip. He could see shadows of the mouth but he still couldn't quite make out the rest of the face. But it had to be Jill. Right?

Then he closed his eyes as the mouth took his cock deep inside. At that moment, he couldn't have cared less who was sucking him with such gusto and such talent. She knew how to drive him almost to coming, then release him and blow on the aching shaft. As he opened his eyes he saw that as she opened her mouth the inside glowed slightly and he could just make out that wonderful tongue.

The woman wrapped her hand around the base of his rod, tightly grasping his shaft, then began sucking again. He felt his come boil in his loins but he couldn't find release with her hand holding him so tightly. He bucked his hips to no avail. "Oh God, I need to come."

He heard a giggle, then a splash and suddenly cold water dribbled over his cock, cooling him only slightly. He heard rustling, then suddenly hands were covering the woman's pussy with the glowing goo. He could see the swollen lips and hear the wet sounds of fingers rubbing a hot, juicy cunt. Oh he wanted that cunt and he struggled to free either his hands or his ankles, but it was no use. He was held securely.

Legs straddled his thighs and that glowing cunt slowly lowered until his cock could feel the radiating heat. He bucked but as his hips jerked upward the cunt stayed just out of reach. Hands pressed him down against the cool wood, then the pussy slowly engulfed his raging hard-on. Down, down, down it pressed taking his entire cock into its heated depths. He could make out the glowing junction of his body and hers and as she rose slightly more of the eerie light was revealed. And again less, then more. He could not only feel their fucking, but he could see it in the increasing and decreasing illumination.

His eyes were riveted on the joining of their bodies.

Then he was beyond anything. His body took over and he thrust upward over and over until spurts of come filled the hot pussy. He tried to remain as silent as she was, but he couldn't restrain his groans as he came again and again.

Finally he collapsed onto the wooden seat, only to feel the pussy withdraw and hands pull up his pants, button his shirt and return him to the way he had been when he entered the Tunnel of Love. The handcuffs were removed from his wrists and ankles and suddenly the boat began to move and the lights returned. He quickly looked around but there was no sign of anyone anywhere. The only sign of what had happened were the two stuffed animals now in the back seat and the pounding of his heart.

He ran his fingers through his hair and, as the boat twisted through the final turns of the ride, he straightened up. What the hell had just happened? He had had the most amazing orgasm of his entire life and he had no real idea who had been responsible. Of course it was Jill.

When the boat stopped, he climbed out, picked up the animals, and looked around, sure he would see Jill waiting for him. There was no one around. He wandered toward the main entrance and, more than fifteen minutes later, he finally found her, tapping her foot. "Where have you been?" Jill asked.

"In the Tunnel of Love like you asked me," he answered.

"I didn't expect you to spend an hour in there. I've been waiting."

"Good act, baby, and I loved it all."

"Loved it all what?"

"You know." He grabbed her and kissed her deeply, pressing his body against her.

She grinned. "Well, whatever it was, I'm for it," she said, returning the kiss and holding him close.

As they left the fair, Greg thought he heard the giggle from somewhere behind him but when he turned there was no one there. And he thought he saw a small glow from beneath Jill's long fingernails but he couldn't really be sure. Oh well. Whatever had happened had been wonderful and it probably didn't pay to delve too deeply into how or why or, most important, who. But if Jill was interested in being the aggressor from time to time, he'd certainly be in favor of it.

Sleigh Ride

"What a fantastic idea," Bev said as her husband Tim tucked the heavy red and blue plaid blanket between her right thigh and the side of the sleigh. "What in the world made you think of it?"

Tim finished making sure the warm blanket was tight across Bev's lap then snuggled against his wife's side and pushed the wooly throw between his thigh and the sleigh. "I saw an ad for this on the lodge's bulletin board and it sounded like a blast."

Bev sighed and watched her breath turn to vapor in the frosty night air. "My nose is freezing, but it's really quite cosy beneath these covers. I'm impressed with your romantic nature."

"Okay, driver," Tim called, grinning. "We're ready."

"I knew there was a reason I married you. You come up with the greatest evenings."

"Well, thank you my dear. Anything for our anniversary."

The horse moved and the sleigh lurched forward then glided smoothly over the snow-packed road, the rhythmic pounding of the hooves making a counterpoint to the jingling of the harness bells. Tim put his arm around Bev's shoulders as the sleigh quickly left the lighted oasis of the ski lodge and headed into the darkened countryside. Twin lanterns rocked softly beside the driver, blackened in the back so as not to illuminate the passengers, yet casting shafts of light along a roadway that the horse obviously knew well. "Look up," Tim said, craning his neck. "I don't think I've ever seen so many stars, certainly not in the city."

Bev leaned her head on Tim's arm. "Me neither. This is so peaceful. And so romantic. God, I love you."

Slowly, Tim's cool lips covered Bev's. The kiss began as a slow exploration, the tip of his tongue teasing her lips and teeth. With a deep sigh, Bev relaxed into the kiss, her tongue dancing with his. As he reached up and cupped the back of her head, she wrapped her arms around his neck. They shifted, deepening the kiss until Bev was breathless. She dropped her head on his arm and he nipped at her earlobe.

"So wonderful," she whispered. "So beautiful. All those stars." She looked around. "Utter blackness with the two of us the only lovers in the world." She cuddled closer, enjoying the feel of the length of his hard body against hers.

"I love you, sexy woman." As they held each other, Tim worked one arm down beneath the blanket and put his hand on Bev's sweatpants-covered thigh, his fingers working their way between them.

The feeling of relaxation was replaced by a rapidly growing heat. "Not here. Let's wait until we get back to our room. Then we can . . ." His fingers were moving toward her mound. She giggled and playfully tried to push her husband's hand away. "Tim, stop." She cupped his cheeks, turned his face toward her, and kissed him again, trying to force down the desire for more. She wasn't going to let Tim get carried away with the driver just a few feet away on his seat. She wasn't that kind of woman. Was she? A sleigh passed going in the other direction, the couple inside laughing.

"Why should we stop?" Tim said, rubbing his cold nose against the side of Bev's neck below her knitted hat. "No one can see."

"Timmy, no," Bev said, her voice not really convincing, his fingers making her moist and hot. Romance was nice, but she loved the way Tim could make her hot so fast. How far could they go? she wondered. This was so, so public. The couldn't, could they? No. Too many clothes. As she thought about it, she realized that, although she was wearing a heavy coat, beneath she was only wearing a sweatshirt, sweatpants, and panties. After a long day of skiing and a hot bath, that was all she wanted to struggle into and the lodge was aggressively informal. She felt Tim's fingers rubbing the insides of her thighs and against her mound. He wouldn't really, would he?

"What do you think I'm going to do?" Tim asked as a sleigh with two couples inside galloped by.

"I know you have an oversexed mind and always wanted to make love in a limo." She looked around. "This looks like the next best thing."

Tim's boyish grin reminded Bev of what she loved about him. "You're right, of course. I knew I couldn't fool you. You also know that I wouldn't do anything to embarrass you. Right?"

Bev sighed. "Right." But his fingers were still rubbing and it was making her wet and hungry.

"No one can see what's going on beneath this lap robe. Right?"

Bev looked down. Everything looked so normal. "Right," she said softly.

"And no one can know what I'm doing, right?" He pressed against her clit.

"Right." Her breathing sped up as his hand continued playing with her. "Timmy, please."

"Please what? If you don't look any different from anyone else taking a sleigh ride, no one will know anything." Another sleigh passed, the couple inside kissing, paying no attention to anyone around them.

Tim's fingers were stroking her clit and it was getting difficult for her to sit still. Slowly, the hand that had been resting on her shoulder moved beneath the covers that were tucked across her breasts. Suddenly she realized that the hand was beneath her sweatshirt, sliding down through the neck opening groping for her nipple. In a hoarse whisper, she said, "Timmy, you really have to stop."

"Do you know that you only call me Timmy when you're excited?"

"I do not." His fingers had found her nipple and were lightly pinching the engorged nubs.

Tim nibbled her ear. "Yes, you do. I always know when you're getting hot. You call me Timmy and your nipples get really hard. Then you can't control your hips and you squirm the delightful way you're wiggling now."

Bev realized that she was moving her entire lower body, trying to get Tim's hands where she wanted them, deep between her legs. She took a deep breath and stopped moving.

"That won't work either," Tim said. "I can hear you breathing hard, making those little noises you make when you're turned on." He pinched her nipple again and she gasped. "See, you can't fool me."

Bev knew that she wasn't going to be able to resist her sexy husband, but two could play the same game. "I guess you're right," she said, twisting slightly toward him on the seat. "Maybe the best defense is a good offense." She fumbled a bit beneath the blanket, then found his hard cock through his sweatpants and squeezed.

"Shit, baby. That's not fair."

"Why not?" she asked, squeezing harder and feeling his cock grow beneath her hand. "Can't two play?" The throb in her pussy caused by his hands grew as she tried to concentrate on manipulating his cock.

There was silence for a few minutes while hands rubbed and played. Tim moved around so that he was facing his wife, then raised her sweatshirt beneath the blanket until her breasts were naked beneath his hands. Bev slipped her fingers through the waistband of his pants and found his naked cock. "You're not wearing any shorts," she said.

"I know us both too well and I hoped this would happen."

"Well, you promised not to embarrass me so be really quiet."

"Yes, ma'am." He smiled, and pinched both nipples. In retaliation, she circled his cock with her fingers and rubbed from tip to base. In silence, she stroked Tim's stiff cock, finding the wetness at the tip then using his own natural lubricant to smooth her path.

Tim slid both hands down her ribs to the waistband of her sweatpants, and beneath. He tunneled downward, realizing that Bev was moving to make the going easier. He found the slender crotch of her panties and wormed a finger underneath. "Oh baby. You're sopping wet."

Bev tipped her pelvis to urge him to penetrate, to ease the heat, to scratch the unbearable itch. She had long since ceased caring about the driver, the passing sleighs, anything outside the blanket. Hunger overwhelmed her and she thought about nothing but Tim and his hands, and his body.

Tim was an expert on exactly where his wife liked to be touched, how to push her upward to ever higher levels, and he drove her to the brink of climax. Then he ducked his head beneath the blanket and took one of her nipples in his mouth. While he inserted two fingers in her hot channel, and rubbed her clit with his other hand, he bit down on Bev's tit.

Struggling to keep from screaming, Bev came, bucking her hips. Quickly, Tim raised his head and covered his wife's mouth with his own, swallowing her whimpers and moans. Panting, barely able to get her breath, Bev slowly came down, her hands still holding Tim's cock.

When she could speak again, she said, "Remember that two can play at this game." She ducked her head beneath the blanket and moved his clothing so she could put her mouth on Tim's cock. As well as Tim knew her body, she knew his. She swirled her tongue around the tip of his erection, running her teeth lightly around the sensitive area just below the head. She tasted his salty juices and felt him tangle his fingers in her hair, holding her head against his groin.

Her hand found his balls and she cupped his testicles, scratching the skin between his balls and his anus. Simultaneously, she sucked the end of his erection into her wet mouth. Still rubbing his perineum, she circled his cock with her other hand and squeezed.

Feeling his semen erupt was one of the most wonderful sensations she could imagine. She felt the pulses in her fingers and felt his warm fluid fill her mouth. Quickly she swallowed, not allowing any of his juices to escape.

Hot and sweating, she slowly pulled her head out from beneath the blanket and they quickly rearranged their clothing and the blanket. As they looked around, they realized that they had reentered the lighted area around the ski lodge and were rapidly approaching the main building.

The sleigh came to a stop and the driver climbed down from his seat to help Bev and Tim out. Tim found his wallet and gave the driver a handsome tip. "Thanks for a wonderful ride," Tim said, as his wife giggled.

The driver winked. "I'm glad you enjoyed it." He motioned to the horse. "If you want to go again, Sadie and I would love to take you." He paused and winked again. "Next time you might want to check out the scenery."

Leaving Bev and Tim laughing, the driver jumped back onto his seat and jingled away.

The Incredible Orgasm Machine

He had put an ad in an underground newspaper near the university, wondering whether everyone who read it would think he was some kind of a nut.

Wanted: A few women to test an orgasm machine. Climaxes guaranteed. Please write to Box 743.

Well maybe he was a nut. A graduate student in advanced computer science, Josh had gotten interested in robotics and, in his spare time, had developed a machine that combined all the sex toys he had ever owned into an integrated orgasm machine. When he had told Janine, his then-girlfriend, about it she had been disgusted. "So that's what you've been tinkering with every night while you were neglecting me. Sex is a people thing. It's not supposed to be computerized." When he had suggested that she try the contraption out, she had made several rude noises, called him a pervert, and stormed out of his apartment, stopping only long enough to grab her clothes and toiletries.

Looking around his now-vacated loft apartment, he sighed. "Well, that's that. I really wanted to try this thing out." He gazed at the softly padded table with its gleaming stainless steel probes and gadgets, all wired into a central computer. "Maybe I should have made something for myself instead."

Josh knew it would take several days for the newspaper to forward any replies to him so he didn't rush to get his mail. No one would trust him enough to let him experiment. No one was that foolish. And even if someone did answer the ad, how could he convince her that he was honest and serious about this work. Even Janine had thought he was weird.

When he got the mail, he was absolutely amazed. There were seven letters from women who wanted more information about his orgasm machine. Seven letters with phone numbers and personal references. Personal references! They were worried about his opinion of them!

He looked through the letters more carefully over the next half hour. He recognized three of the names, women with whom he had taken classes; two were computer science graduate students like himself.

The one he settled on for a first contact was named Shelly.

A short, well-built blonde, she had ordinary features but a great sense of humor and a quick mind. And, to the best of his knowledge, she had recently broken up with her football-player-type boyfriend. "I would love to help you with your experiments," she had written. "Just name the time and place."

That evening, Josh called Shelly. "Hi," he said, feeling a bit awkward. "I'm Josh McAllister. We took Hodgsen's computer networking class together last semester."

"Oh, sure. I remember you," she said, her voice soft, her attitude curious.

"Well, I'm the one who put the ad in the Distorter," he said, using the common nickname of the newspaper.

"I should have guessed. You've always had a delightfully perverse mind. Have you really invented an orgasm machine? You've got me so curious."

Ah Shelly, Josh thought, you've got me so much more than curious. He could feel his cock swell beneath his jeans. This had begun as a scientific project but was rapidly becoming something quite a bit more. Maybe this could be the beginning of something terrific.

They arranged to meet at one of the campus coffee shops and together, over several cappuccinos, he explained his project. "Can the computer really establish orgasmic thresholds so that climax would go on and on?"

"In theory, yes. But Janine didn't want to test it out, so I haven't any real data to go on."

"Well," Shelly said, her eyes wide, her pupils already dilated, "I would love to."

Mentally shaking his head at his good fortune, Josh led the way to his loft. Shelly gazed at the large open space. "This is really nice," she said, her voice faltering slightly.

"Listen, if you're nervous about this, we can call it off at any time."

Shelly took a deep breath. "No, not nervous. I couldn't do this with anyone I didn't already know. I mean, it's so personal, and a bit embarrassing."

Josh grinned. "Me too. Now that you're here and all, it seems a bit weird. Maybe Janine was right. Maybe I am a pervert."

"Don't be silly, you're not at all." She patted his cheek and smiled at him. "Should we kiss or something?"

"No. The best experiment I can think of is for you to start cold, as it were." He could actually feel the color rise in his cheeks. He was blushing. This was so silly. "Let's look at it as science."

Shelly winked at him. "Not a chance, but I'll try to keep my thoughts out of the gutter."

Josh laughed. "Okay. This is bizarre. I'll admit it."

"Maybe we should have a beer first, or something."

"I'd rather you were totally sober. It's better for the experiment." He paused. "You need to be naked. Maybe you should go into the bathroom." He reached into a drawer of his dresser and pulled out a tailored shirt. "Put this on and then I'll show you the machine."

Minutes later, as Josh typed a few commands into the central computer, Shelly came out of the bathroom, Josh's shirt wrapped around her. "Okay, now what?" she asked.

"Lie down here," Josh said, indicating the softly padded leather table. As Shelly climbed onto the table, he caught a quick glimpse of her pale bush. A real blonde, he thought, unscientifically. "Now, I need to fasten these blood pressure cuffs around both your arms and both your thighs."

Shelly looked at the four wide bands and nodded. Quickly, Josh pushed the shirt sleeves up, Velcroed the arm straps closed. He tried not to gaze at her soft, white skin as he attached the matching bands to her upper thighs. He pumped them all up until they were just snug, then attached other sensing devices to her wrists and ankles. With her cooperation, he wrapped a snug band, with wires extending from it, around her waist against her skin, finding it more and more difficult to remain objective at the vision of her sexy body. "Now we get down to it, I guess," he said. "I need to unbutton the shirt."

Again Shelly nodded and he quickly parted the sides of the shirt to reveal her rose-tipped breasts. "These are suckers," he explained, "attached to suction devices activated by the computer. The sensing devices will measure your responses and react accordingly." He spread Vaseline over the cups and pressed them over Shelly's slightly erect nipples. "How does that feel?"

"Actually it's kind of kinky. I'm getting a little turned on by this whole thing."

"It's important that you tell me things like that, although it's not the machine yet." He moved to the keyboard and typed in a command.

As Shelly lay on the table, she wondered what she had gotten herself into. Sure, Josh was really cute, in a country-boyish way, with his floppy sandy hair and his cute eyes, covered with those adorable glasses. But this was a bit much. And what could an orgasm machine do, anyway. Good sex was the only real way to hot climaxes, and she had had her share. Except for Josh's cute blushes whenever he looked at her body, this was sort of impersonal. It would never work.

Suddenly there was a sucking at her breasts, slow and deep, just the way she liked her tits sucked. "Oooh," Shelly said, "that's really good." Good, it was wonderful, causing darts of pleasure to prickle through her.

"At first it might feel a bit strange as the machine experiments to find your ideal levels of pleasure. Be patient."

The sucking intensified, then softened. At one point the pulling became almost unpleasant, but it quickly settled into a depth and rhythm that made her blood heat. "Mmm, that's really good."

"Great. It's established your thresholds of pleasure and discomfort. It should continue at exactly the right level." As he left her alone for a few moments she relaxed and let the suckers draw the pleasure out. It was dynamite.

"Shall we move on?" Josh asked.

"Mmm," was all Shelly wanted to say. Then she felt something cool and slippery slide through the folds of her slit, then slowly delve inside of her. It seemed to grow and swell to fill her completely as Josh fastened its straps around her hips. "Oh," she said as the device moved inside of her. Something inside the sleeve was touching every part of her channel.

"It's sensing all the spots that feel the best, whether G-spots or whatever. Then it will stroke you in all the right places."

Now Shelly had the pulling on her breasts and the rubbing of the device inside her. Slowly her hips began to move in rhythm with the machines controlling her. "Now this," Josh said, placing a warm pad against her clit and fastening it to the straps that held the dildo in place. The pad rubbed and moved against her clitoris, urging her higher. Just when she thought she would climax, the movements changed to more gentle stroking so she slowly came down. When she reflexively reached to rub herself, Josh held her wrists. "Let the machine do it. You won't be disappointed."

"But . . ."

"Let me fasten your wrists so you can't do anything to help yourself. Please. Do you trust me? It will be so good."

Shelly hesitated, then decided to trust Josh and his orgasm machine. At her nod, Josh fastened two straps around her wrists then hooked them to the sides of the table. "Is it still good?"

Shelly sighed. "Yes. It's good, but I was so close there for a moment."

"I know, but the machine's designed to make it last. Shall we go for the full treatment?"

Shelly only hesitated for a moment. "Go for it," she said.

Slowly the machine drove her higher, then she felt Josh urge her knees up. Resting her feet on the table, Shelly obliged, then felt something cold and slick rub against her rear hole. "I've never done anything like this before," she said. "Maybe it's too much."

She heard Josh type something into the computer and the suckers changed their rhythm. The dildo and pad also adjusted so she was flying again. She wanted, needed. She was close, but not close enough. Again the cold implement rubbed her anus, but this time she didn't ask to stop. Slowly a slender rod pressed into her and lodged itself in her rear passage. A ring around the end rubbed the tender skin of her opening, lightly massaging her in a place no one had ever touched before.

She was only moments away from the best orgasm of her life and again the machines caused her to slip away. "No," she said, frustrated. "Please."

• • •

Josh could take it no longer. His cock was so hard from watching Shelly thrash around on the table that he unzipped his pants and allowed it to spring free. As he stroked it, he felt Shelly's gaze on him. "This isn't too scientific," he said, "but you make me so hot."

Shelly smiled, then licked her lips. "I can help, if it won't ruin the experiment." She licked her lips again.

"Oh God," Josh said. He typed something into the computer and the legs of the table slowly retracted until Shelly's head was level with his crotch. Then he set the machine to keep her at the top of her excitement, just before climax, took a hand-held controller, and moved beside her. She smiled, licked her lips and opened her mouth. He slowly thrust his swollen cock into her mouth, holding her head with both hands. As he fucked her mouth, he knew the machine was giving her perfect sexual pleasure. She could hardly hold still as the machines worked at her body and his cock worked in her mouth.

As he felt come boil from his belly, he pressed a key on the controller in his hand and knew that in about five seconds the machine would drive her over the edge. Thus, moments later, they climaxed simultaneously.

Josh collapsed in a chair and for several minutes the only sound in the room was their slowly calming breathing.

"Holy shit," Shelly said, Josh's come still coating her chin. "Holy shit."

"It was really good, wasn't it?"

"It was the best orgasm I've ever had. That machine should sell for millions of dollars."

Josh couldn't control the big grin on his face. "It worked just as I thought it would. I'm a genius."

"Are you enough of a genius to make one for men too?"

"With your help, of course."

"Absolutely. And I'm sure there will be lots of need for experimentation."

The Incredible Orgasm Machine: Josh's Turn

Shelly and Josh had been working together for several weeks, perfecting the ultimate orgasm machine. Not that it needed perfecting, Shelly thought, but she didn't share her thoughts with Josh. She loved the tinkering and the experimentation. She'd had more earth-shattering orgasms in the past few weeks than she'd had in her entire life. God, science was wonderful.

Finally they had decided to begin work on the male version of the machine. "This is really embarrassing," Josh said the first morning.

"Well, it was for me at first too, if you remember. Just think of all the money we can make with the two machines." She raised an eyebrow and giggled. "It will put massage parlors totally out of business."

"Okay," Josh said with a sigh. "I'll concentrate on the money."

"Right. Of course you will," Shelly said sarcastically. "Now, where do we begin?"

"I guess we need to calibrate the machine, establish norms of male arousal."

"Okay. How did you do that for the female program?"

"Actually, I guessed at the pulse, respiration, and skin responses. Janine taught me about wetness and clitoral and nipple erections."

"Your ex participated in your experiments?"

"Don't be ridiculous. She had no idea what I was doing. I just paid attention while we made love and afterward I wrote down details then translated them into the proper parameters."

Shelly snorted. "You must have been dynamite in bed. Equations. Yuch." Shelly studied Josh. Strangely enough, with all their sexual experimentation they remained colleagues and little more. Although she wanted to change that, Josh seemed content. For the moment, Shelly thought.

"No judgments please," Josh said. "Let's use the same pulse, respirations, and skin responses as the female version uses. Of course, clitoral and nipple responses are out."

"Your nipples don't get hard like mine?"

"Men's nipples don't get erect," Josh pronounced.

I wonder, Shelly thought. "If this is to be a true test, it's important for you to keep your hands off your cock."

"I have amazing self-control when I want to," Josh said.

Sometimes he's such a pompous ass, she thought, but he's so cute. "Let's just see what we can adapt. Why don't you get naked and then we can judge what more we need to do?"

"Okay," Josh said and began to remove his clothes.

Aside from the frequent sessions of fellatio, Shelly had had little sexual contact with Josh and she had never seen him naked. He has a great body, Shelly realized, but she was sad at the ease with which he dropped his clothing. He obviously thought of her as a partner in his research, not a woman. Well, she'll see what she could do about that.

Naked, Josh lay down on the padded table and Shelly attached the blood pressure cuffs to his arms and thighs. She watched his cock twitch slightly as her hand brushed his skin, but it remained relatively flaccid. How the hell could he take this all so calmly?

"I don't think this will do much in its current state," Josh said, answering Shelly's unspoken question. "It will undoubtedly take a bit of tinkering and maybe a few new toys, too."

"Well, we'll do the best we can with what we've got." She lightly inflated the cuffs, then fastened the other sensors to check his skin and breathing. "Let's start with the nipples. If they aren't sensitive, the machine can establish its first set of nonaroused levels." Shelly greased the suckers and placed them on his hairless chest. Josh had shown her how to control the computer program so Shelly quickly clicked a few keys.

As she watched his face, Josh's eyes closed. "That feels really nice," he said. "I guess it is sort of sexy."

The machine's sucking increased, then decreased, slowly conditioning his nipples. Eventually, Shelly reasoned, they would become as erogenous as other parts of his body. She had learned quite a lot about human sexuality in her weeks of working with Josh. She had read his texts, with special attention to the male responses, to which, she discovered, he paid little mind. Many men had nipples as sensitive as a woman's if only they were properly stimulated.

Josh's cock stirred and Shelly smiled. "Josh, remember my first time?"

It seemed to take a moment for Josh to refocus his attention. "Yeah, sure. What about it?"

Shelly noticed his breathing rate had increased and the computer was adjusting the suction on the nipple pads. "Well, you had to control my hands. I think we should keep this test totally free from any outside influences."

"Meaning?"

Rather than answering, Shelly merely took each of Josh's wrists and fastened them to the sides of the table. "Good. Now let's play." Shelly lubricated Josh's entire groin area, then took the pad that usually covered her clit and slowly wrapped it around his testicles. It took a bit of fiddling but she finally got it to stay in place without touching his semierect cock. Then she clicked a few computer keys and the vibrations began.

"Shit, Shelly. That's too much."

"Leave it to the machine," she purred. "Let it find your levels." She watched Josh's cock harden and his body tremble. Soon she could tell from the computer's screen that it had found just the right combination of pressure and vibration to bring him to full arousal.

"I'm not sure I like this," he said. "It's like fucking a machine."

"It is fucking a machine, or being fucked by one. It's going to become the ultimate sex toy. Relax, baby, and just roll with it."

"God, Shell, it's hard."

Shelly looked at his cock, sticking straight up from his crotch. "I know," she giggled. "It's difficult when you realize that it's not another person, but rather pieces of metal and plastic. But it's really kinky too. I should know."

Josh shuddered and Shelly knew his attention was entirely focused on his cock and balls. She found another clitoral pad, connected it to the computer, held it in her hand, and touched his cock. She watched the indicators on the computer screen so as not to cause him to climax too quickly. She varied her pressure according to the readouts. "God, you're so close," she whispered.

"Shelly," he cried. "Shelly!"

She released him. The stimulation levels were getting too high and he was in danger of ejaculating. Not just yet, she told herself. She raised his knees and lubricated the anal probe.

"Shelly, no. Don't do that. I'm not into anal sex. It will only spoil the whole thing."

She watched the levels on the machine. His voice was telling her no, but he was obviously very excited too. "Let's just give it a try and see what happens. I wasn't keen on the idea either at first."

"Shelly, no. This is a really bad idea." He struggled but the wrist straps held tight.

"Be a sport. I'll watch the computer and I won't do anything you don't enjoy." She saw that his muscles were tightly clenched but the computer changed the levels of stimulation on his cock and balls and slowly he relaxed and his cheeks parted. Quickly, before he had time to react, she slipped the slender rod an inch into his ass.

"Shit, Shelly. Stop!"

"The computer says Don't Stop, and I'm going to believe it rather than you for now." Slowly she pressed the rod in deeper and then left it in place. She watched as the indicators told her the vibrations in the rod were increasing. She clicked a few keys and his arousal level rose to the edge of orgasm. Then she told the computer to keep him right there.

"I've been dreaming of this moment," she purred as she removed her clothes. She climbed onto the table, positioning her pussy above his face. "Now I want you to suck me. No machine, just your mouth, your tongue." She could feel his breath on her heated flesh. "Do it, baby."

"God, Shelly. Yes."

She lowered her cunt onto his mouth and almost screamed when she felt his tongue caressing her sopping body. "Do it," she cried and he did. She felt him use all the things the computer had taught him about her body, the spots that drove her crazy, the exact pressures and rhythms. But this was so much better. This was his hot mouth and tongue bringing her to climax. "Oh, yes, Josh. Oh yes!"

As she felt her climax approaching, she pressed the remote computer control and the program responded, causing them to climax together. Then she collapsed on top of him and the computer screen went dark. "That was amazing," Josh said, long minutes later as his breathing and pulse slowed.

"I know," Shelly said, giggling, unfastening his wrists.

"It will only take a few minor adjustments to the pads and such to make this work for both sexes." When Shelly rose onto her knees and cuffed him on the hip, he laughed and continued, "You are fabulous, sex is fabulous. The machine is an adjunct, a sex toy."

Shelly thought a minute. Great sex was whatever it wanted to be—machine, Josh, whatever! "Let's not be too hasty here," she said. "It will take lots of sessions to get it just right."

"Oh yes," he said, enfolding her in his arms. "Lots of experimentation."

Couch Potato

Marty was a baseball fan. His wife, Tina, didn't really mind
since she enjoyed reading and Marty's devotion to the TV
gave her time to devour the mystery novels she so enjoyed.
When she complained, which she did occasionally, Marty
would turn off the game and do whatever she wanted.

The Mets were playing a day game on the west coast and
the Yankees were at home in the evening. So, with a game at
4:00 and another at 7:00, Tina and a couple of friends had
decided to celebrate with a girls' night out. By the time she
returned home at about 9:00, she was more than a little tipsy.
And she was horny. The four women had talked a great deal
about sex, lamenting the creativity that seemed to be seeping

slowly from their respective marriages. The creativity's not gone from my marriage, Tina had maintained, but deep inside she wasn't so sure.

"Hi hon," Marty said as Tina closed the front door behind her.

"Hi love," Tina said. "How's the game going?"

"Mets won but the Yankees are losing one-nothing in the fifth. It's a real pitcher's duel. Oakland's pitcher's . . ."

Tina fuzzed out, not hearing Marty's recitation. God, she was hungry for Marty's body. What the hell was she going to do about it? She could ask for some time with her husband, but she didn't want the usual. Creativity. She faded back in when Marty said, "You gonna read?"

"I don't know right now. You just relax and enjoy. Need anything from the kitchen?" What did she want?

"Nah. I'm fine."

Tina wandered into the kitchen and poured herself a beer. As she swallowed, she thought, I need my husband. Now! She remembered the days before they were married. Ripping each other's clothes off. Lots of kissing, touching, oral sex. God, she remembered how good Marty tasted, how much she had always enjoyed licking and sucking him. A few times he had even come in her mouth. She shook her head. It had been a long time.

In the living room she gazed at her husband lounging on the couch in front of the TV, feet up, body relaxed, beer on the floor near his hand. A grin spread across her face. Why not?

Beer in hand, she crossed the living room and sat on the floor beside Marty's thighs. "Gonna watch with me?" Marty asked. "Great game. Yankees have three hits, and Oakland's got five."

"Just pay no attention to me," Tina said. She rested her head against the edge of the sofa cushion and took another swig of her beer, setting her glass down beside Marty's. Slowly she turned her head and stared at the crotch of her husband's jeans. What the fuck? She reached up and slowly pulled down her husband's zipper.

"What are you doing?" Marty asked although it was perfectly obvious what she was doing.

"I just told you to pay no attention to me," Tina said, with another grin. She reached into the opening in Marty's pants, parted the fly of his shorts, and freed his flaccid cock. Small, soft, just waiting for some fun.

"Hey. I can't 'just pay no attention' when you do something like that," Marty said, his complaint softened by his husky tone and the gleam in his eye.

"You just watch your game and let me play mine." She could feel her pussy moisten and the lips swell.

Tina watched Marty's eyes as he stared at her, smiled, then returned his gaze to the TV. She knew that he wasn't paying attention to the baseball game anymore. Her game kept his attention focused on his crotch. She felt his excitement as his cock hardened in reaction to her warm fingers encircling his member. She watched her long red nails as her fingers stroked and petted. She heard Marty's breathing get coarse and irregular. "Watch your game," she said again.

She climbed onto her knees, placing her mouth at the level of his crotch. Oh God, how she remembered. A small pearl of pre-come oozed from the tip of his now-hard cock. She encircled his dick with her fist, pushing down from head to base, tightening the skin over the end. She licked her lips and extended her tongue.

She heard his gasp as she licked the oozing drop from the tip of his erection. She covered the head with small kisses then licked as if it were an all-day sucker. "Oh baby," Marty groaned.

"You're paying attention to me. You're supposed to be watching the game."

"Yeah, right," Marty said his voice hoarse.

Tina giggled, then made an "O" with her lips and took the head of his cock into her warm, wet mouth. With her hand around the base, she pushed her mouth down over the tight skin. She knew she couldn't "deep throat" like the movies, but between the pressure of her fist and the slight suction of her mouth, she knew Marty couldn't have cared less.

"Oh baby," Marty said again. "That's so great."

Tina pulled back, then took him deep again. Over and over, she pulled and thrust, feeling his hips buck.

"If you keep doing that, I'll come in your mouth," Marty moaned.

"And the problem with that is?"

"Shit baby."

She sucked, imitating the motions of intercourse. Again and again, until she felt the pumping at the base of his penis. She knew he was ready, and she almost came herself just from the pure pleasure of his arousal. She wanted to rub her pussy but didn't because she knew that Marty wouldn't allow her to remain unsatisfied.

She felt the spasms in her fingers as he erupted. She opened her mouth wide, allowing it to fill with his fluids, relishing the salty, tangy taste. She swallowed his come and took a deep breath.

"Oh shit, darling," Marty said, still panting. "What came over you?"

"I just got to thinking about how it was back when we were first married. I kind of miss that mad passion."

"I didn't realize how much I missed it too." He pressed a button and the TV went dark. "Let's go to bed and see what else I remember. I vaguely recall how much you enjoyed it when I licked your pussy."

"Umm. I vaguely recall that too." Together they walked into the bedroom and made love for another hour.

Telling Tales

"She was amazing," Jarred said, "long blonde hair, gorgeous face, fabulous body. I didn't measure, but she must have been at least a 34DD. Gigantic knockers with dark brown nipples just begging for my mouth." He winked at his three buddies and sipped his beer. "If you know what I mean."

"Jarred, you're such a lying sack of shit," Pete said, grabbing a handful of peanuts from the bowl in the center of the table. "A different fantastic girl each week? Not a fuckin' chance."

"Not a chance in hell," Mark said, wiping his mouth with the back of his hand. "I, for one, am not interested in listening to your dream-girl stories anymore."

"Me neither," Adam echoed. "Not another tale. I'm tired of it all."

Jarred looked around the table. Well, it could have happened just the way he had said. "She was really fabulous," he said, a bit hesitantly.

"Right," Mark said. "And I'm Brad Pitt."

Jarred had been embellishing his lackluster sex life with stories like this for several months. What the hell, he reasoned. Why not? He was just bringing a little juicy sex into an otherwise dull evening. Sure, he liked the guys and they talked about their girls too. They probably dressed their stories up with a little splash, so why shouldn't he? "It's really true, guys. Really."

"Not another word," Mark said. "Ever. If you meet Jennifer Lopez in the parking lot and fuck her brains out in the backseat of your car, I, for one, don't want to hear about it. Period."

"Me neither," the two other college students echoed.

Jarred slumped back in his chair as the conversation moved on to other topics. His sex life was in the toilet and now he couldn't even make up his little fantasies. He sighed, lifted his mug and tuned in to his buddies' talk about their recent English Lit assignment.

Three days later, on a hot May afternoon, as he was leaving the supermarket after picking up some necessities, like beer and corn chips, he spotted a nice-looking female, trying to start her junk-mobile of a car. He dumped his groceries in his trunk, then, seeing the girl still having difficulties, walked over. "Can I give you a hand?"

Close up, she was even better than he could have imagined. She was a redhead, with curls that tumbled partway down her back. Her eyes were deep blue, with long lashes. Her lips were colored deep red, with a bitable lower one. Since she was behind the wheel, he couldn't see her body, but it was probably just as fantastic as her face. She was a wet dream come true.

"Oh, well maybe," she said, her voice pitched low and sexy. "I don't know anything about cars and I'm afraid this piece of junk has finally given up the ghost."

Jarred knew little more than the girl did about cars but, trying to look knowledgeable, he opened the hood and peered at the engine. Looks like a dirty, oily engine to me, he thought. "I don't really know too much but from the sound as I walked up, I think you're going to need a mechanic to get anywhere." He considered a moment, then asked, "Can I give you a lift somewhere?"

She seemed to ponder, then said, "Actually, if you wouldn't mind. I've got ice cream and lots of frozen stuff in the backseat and I can almost hear it melting. I'll get someone to have a look at the car later. I'm visiting a friend for the day. She lives just a few blocks from here and I bought a few things for when she gets home from work."

Shit, Jarred thought. It don't get much better than this. "Sure. Let me bring my car over and we'll transfer your bags."

A few moments later, Jarred pulled his car up next to the junker and started to open the back door. "I'm Mandy," the girl said as she climbed from behind the wheel.

"Jarred," he mumbled, staring. She was even more gorgeous standing up. Short shorts revealed long, shapely legs and her tight crop-top barely covered her voluptuous chest. As he fumbled with the trunk lid, she leaned against him.

"You'll never be able to open that. Let me." She reached for the key, giving his arm a good feel of her pillowy breasts. "It's a big pain." She wiggled the key in the lock, pushed, then pulled, all the time pressing herself against his arm and chest. His pants could barely contain his erection.

"There," she said as the lid flipped open. Wordlessly they transferred her groceries to the backseat of Jarred's SUV. She told him her address and they drove the few blocks in silence, with Jarred trying desperately to think of something to say. He pulled up to the curb and switched the engine off. "Uh, can I help you with the bags?"

"Sure, if you wouldn't mind." The apartment was small but comfortable and they quickly set all the bags on the tiny kitchen counter. Jarred couldn't keep his eyes off the girl's breasts as she leaned and stretched, putting the frozen food into the freezer. "I can't thank you enough," she said. "You saved my life." She smiled. "Well, at least you saved my ice cream." Then she leaned up and kissed him on the cheek. "Thanks."

"You're w-w-welcome," he stammered.

She cupped his face in her palms and pressed her lips against his. A long kiss and lots of tongue later, she pulled back. "That's a better thank you." Then she reached down and grasped his immense hard-on. "I'd like to thank you even more."

He couldn't believe his eyes, or his dick. She was actually rubbing and squeezing him through his shorts. This was some kind of fantasy come true. With one motion, he grabbed the bottom of her shirt and pulled it over her head. Her breasts were covered with tiny bits of cream-colored lace, large brown nipples pressing forward. Quickly he pinched the tips, then bent and took one in his mouth. "Ummm," she purred, her hand still manipulating his cock. "You're quite something. Let's go inside."

How they got naked, Jarred couldn't figure out, but soon they were on her bed, the full length of her body pressed against his. "Touch me here," she said, placing his hand between her legs. She was sopping wet and so slippery. He wanted to climb over her and ram himself home, but the feel of his fingers rubbing her sweet pussy was incredibly delicious. She put her hand over his and guided him to all her secret places. "Yes," she moaned. "Like that."

He'd touched his share of girls, but now she was showing him just the way she liked it. She was actually using his fingers to masturbate and it was heaven. "Oh, yes," she moaned again, her hips bucking and rolling. "Right there . . . So good . . . Yes, finger-fuck me." He drove three fingers into her slippery channel, rubbing and thrusting. "Now rub here. Don't stop! Don't stop!"

Then he felt her come, spasms on his fingers, copious amounts of fluid spilling down his hand. He'd never felt anything like it.

"Now fuck me hard," she said, quickly pulling a condom from her bed-table drawer and unrolling it onto his rock-hard pole. She climbed on top of him and rammed his cock into her pussy. Although she had asked him to fuck her, she did all the work, rising and dropping onto his cock until she screamed, "Yes, yes!" Again he could feel the tight pussy-spasms and he could hold back no longer. With a thrust of his hips, he came, groaning and grinding his body against hers.

Later she dropped against his chest, panting. "Wow. That was great," she said.

"Was it ever!"

Moments later, while he was still catching his breath, she dressed and handed him his pants. "Listen," she said, "I've got to see about my car. But thanks so much for the ride, and," she leered and winked, "for the ride."

Jarred pulled on his pants and shirt, then slipped into his sneakers. "That was truly amazing," he said. "When can I see you again?"

"I'm not really sure," she said, guiding him to the door. "Why don't you call me?"

"Okay." He was barely through the door when he heard it close behind him.

He relived every moment as he drove back to his room. He'd never been fucked like that before and Mandy would fill his dreams until the next time he could see her. Mandy. Mandy what? He couldn't remember her last name. Had she told him? Phone her? He didn't know her name and hadn't noticed her address. Shit. No way!!! He had no way to get in touch with her, and now he understood that she had never intended him to contact her again.

Well, easy come, easy go. He laughed to himself at his unintentional pun. He dropped onto the bed. The guys. He had to tell the guys. He reached for the phone then stopped. They'd never believe him. His story would be just like all his other tales. Shit!

Wait a minute. Had this been a setup? Had they arranged this with the girl so he would tell his tale and they would claim not to believe him? Either way, he couldn't tell them, or anyone. It would have to be his secret. But damn, what a secret!

At a Bar

I was sitting in a rear-corner booth in my favorite neighborhood watering hole when she walked in. God she was sexy. Not especially attractive, but sexy as hell. She had an average figure, but her clothes said it all. She was wearing a tight black blouse, unbuttoned one button too far, and a tight black skirt that came to just above her knees. Her black stockings accented nice legs that ended in drop-dead shoes with four-inch heels. Quite a few heads turned, including a few regulars who don't look at just anyone.

It was only after dwelling on her body that I got to her face, pretty, with deep blue eyes, and lots of red lipstick. Her dark brown hair was loose and fell to her shoulders. My eyes wandered over the entire package. No one part would stop traffic, but put together . . . The package said FUCK ME. And my cock noticed. Oh yes it did.

She sat down at the bar and her skirt slid up her thighs. I'm sure I caught just a glimpse of the lacy top of her stocking before she pulled it down again. Funny, at the time I thought her motions didn't say what her outfit said. She seemed a bit nervous and, after ordering a drink, she looked around, watching the door. She was waiting for someone. Shit. Too bad.

I watched her glance at her watch, then stare at the door, constantly stirring her drink but sipping only occasionally. Maybe he's not coming, I thought. Maybe there's a chance . . .

I grabbed my beer and started to rise, only to have my hopes dashed. A man appeared at the door of the bar and my lady's face lit up. He was the one she had been waiting for, more's the pity. Dressed in a sports jacket and slacks, he was the picture of a yuppie stock trader; the lucky bastard looked around, then spotted her at the bar. He walked over and sat down beside her.

Now the bar's not too large and it's not like I was eavesdropping or anything. I could just hear what they were saying. "Hi, sweet thing," he said. "Come here often? Can I buy you a drink?"

Just like that. She'd been waiting for him for fifteen minutes but he sounded like he was picking her up. And what a corny line. I looked him over. Now I'm no gorgeous guy, but he had nothing on me. Glasses, shaggy haircut. Big ears. Why him? And what the hell was going on?

"I have a drink," she said.

"Great. I'll just have one with you." He ordered a glass of red wine. Red wine. What a wussy. "Let's sit somewhere more private," he said and they moved to the booth behind mine. I took a swallow of my beer and felt the two sit with their backs against the back of my seat.

They made small talk for several minutes, with me listening to every word. Her voice was soft, like the melody of a song. Listen to me sounding like a poet, but her voice was like poetry. His voice was cultured, with maybe a slight British accent.

"You know, you're a sexy thing," he said and she laughed softly. "I love the way your breasts fill out that blouse. I can see down the front." There was a rustling, then she said, "Stop that," but she didn't sound too convincing.

"I like it down there," he said. "I can feel your tits pressing against my fingers."

He had stuffed his fingers down the front of that blouse. God, I wished I had my fingers down the front of that blouse, feeling her boobs. My cock wished that too. Oh well.

"Now baby, stop," she whispered. "People can see."

"No one can see anything," he said. "And anyway, who cares? We'll never be in here again. Who cares who sees what?"

She giggled again. "If that's the way you want to play it."

Then I heard him gasp. Had she grabbed his crotch? That's sure the way it sounded.

"You're playing with fire," he said, the warning in his voice softened by his gentle laugh.

"I hope so," she said softly. Then she gasped. I wondered what he had done. "Stop it," she said, her breathing quick and hard. "You'll pop the buttons if your keep doing that, and I just bought this blouse." Both the guy and I could tell she wasn't really complaining.

His hands must have been filled with her tits. Reflexively I cupped my hands as though filled with large globes of heated flesh. I could almost feel her breasts in my palms, her nipples hard and erect. I closed my eyes and listened to her heavy breathing.

"Slide your skirt up until you're sitting directly on the seat," he ordered and I heard rustling and felt the booth seat shift. "Now slide your panties off."

"Bob," she said. "Not here." Her protest was halfhearted at best.

"Yes, here. Right here."

I heard her sigh, then the booth shifted again. Shit. I could picture it. She was getting naked, her gorgeous pussy hidden by the table but open to the man's gaze. Her thighs would be so white over the tops of her black stockings. I thought about how beautiful her cunt must be, dark curly hair to match the deep brown hair on her head, soft pink pussy-flesh peeking out through her bush.

"Shit," she hissed. He must be touching her, I thought. Running his fingers through her hair, between her sopping pussy-lips. Oh yes, they would be open and so wet. I rubbed my fingers across the edge of the table, imitating the man's motions. My cock was making me really uncomfortable jammed in my tight jeans. Well, if he could do it, what was stopping me? I unzipped my jeans and adjusted my hard-on to a more comfortable position, centered in the opening.

"Oh baby," she purred. "Keep doing that."

"Only if you do me too." I heard the sound of a zipper and then his gasp. "You've got great hands," he said. "Baby . . ."

I couldn't resist. I parted the fly of my shorts and my hard cock sprang free. Pre-come had oozed from the tip and I rubbed it around my cock-head.

"Rub up and down," he said, and I felt the rhythmic motions through the back of my seat. They were actually jacking each other off right there in the booth, not two feet behind my head.

"Don't you stop either," she panted.

Don't either of you stop, I thought, rubbing the length of my cock, knowing it wouldn't be long before I spurted.

For several long moments there was little sound, just lots of heavy breathing, some of it mine. The booth rocked softly as we all took our pleasure, them hand-fucking each other and me picturing her hands on my dick.

"Shit," she hissed again. "Shit. Baby . . ."

"Yessss."

Me too. I came right there. In my favorite bar. Right there in my usual booth. Thank God none of my friends were there and thank God again for the dim lighting. I actually jacked myself off in a booth in a bar. I must be some kind of a pervert, but it felt so good that I quickly decided not to worry about it.

"That was amazing," she said. "I never believed it would be so hot."

"It was a great idea."

"Yeah. Let's hear it for planned spontaneity."

"What's on for next Saturday night?" he said, his breathing now almost normal.

"You get to pick. I picked this week's."

"Did you tell Audrey we wanted her for next Saturday as well?"

"I did. Will you drive her home while I check on the kids?"

"Sure, but then get into bed and let's see whether we can finish this evening the best way."

There was more movement and then they were gone. A date. They had kids. This was a sex game. I sighed. What a great game.

I Love Sunshine

Have you ever made love in the sunshine? Well, let me tell you I was never the type to do it on a beach or golf course and I'm still not. However, and that's a big however, my husband Wayne and I had the opportunity to make love with the sun shining on our bodies last winter and it was fabulous. Let me give you the details.

Wayne and I go on vacation each winter. We live in the northeast and it's freezing here. We both hate the cold, and snow and ice make it even worse. So, to make the season pass more quickly, we always take a week in February and get away to someplace warm. Okay, it's a bit indulgent, but we need it and, since we both have good jobs, we can afford it.

This past winter we decided to give Southern California a try and after some information gathering, we picked Palm Springs. Ever been there? We hadn't so we read brochures and haunted the internet until we found the least expensive flight and an inexpensive rental car. As we were browsing, we stumbled upon a website devoted to a hotel that was actually a collection of modern bungalows with views of the mountains. It was a bit pricey, but the posted photos looked so good that we decided to spend a little extra and made reservations.

We flew into L.A. and then drove the three hours to Palm Springs so we arrived well after dark. Our little cottage was lovelier than we had imagined, all white inside, walls, furniture, everything. The only color were the drapes and bedspread, which were covered with huge bright yellow sunflowers and green leaves. Three walls of the cabin were mostly windows with louvers that could be closed for privacy or opened to what we were told was a spectacular view of the desert.

Since we were pretty tired, we went out to get a quick bite of dinner then returned to our room and crashed. We hadn't thought to close the drapes and the louvers were partially open so the following morning we were awakened to a room filled with sunshine. I flipped back the light blanket and sheet we had been sleeping under and stretched out like a cat in the warmth.

"You look very sexy that way," Wayne said, sleepily.

I wiggled my hips, enjoying the feel of the soft cotton sheets on my back and the sun on my front. I was wearing only my usual satin pajamas and Wayne had on a pair of briefs. Knowing Wayne was probably thinking what he usually thinks in the morning, I asked, "How private are we?"

Wayne sat up and looked around, then got up and flipped the louvers closed on one wall, but left the other two open. He climbed back into bed beside me and said, "Now all I see is desert and mountains beyond. As long as we don't worry about coyotes and jackrabbits, we're pretty private."

"Wonderful," I said, opening the front of my pajamas. The louvers on the wall of windows at the foot of the bed were wide open and, since we faced east, the morning sun speared through the glass. Almost immediately I felt the heat on my skin and my nipples puckered from the warmth.

"You like the feel of that?" Wayne asked, his hand stroking my abdomen.

"Umm," I purred, rather like a cat with a bowl of cream. "This feels so decadent."

"You're beautiful in the sun," Wayne said. "You look like some kind of pagan goddess." He grabbed my pajama bottoms by the elastic waist and pulled them off. "Spread your legs and feel it on your pussy."

I did, and the sensation immediately made me hot. Hot from the sun, and incredibly hot from the inside out. Wayne discovered that one of the glass panels at the foot of the bed was really a sliding door and he quickly dragged it open so the unfiltered light shone on me. My internal and external temperature rose about ten degrees. Man, I was boiling.

"Come here and lie next to me," I purred. "And take off those silly shorts."

Wayne pulled off his briefs and stretched out beside me. I could tell by his almost immediate erection that the sun was having the same effect on him as it had on me. "Feels hedonistic, doesn't it?"

"God," Wayne said. "This is dynamite."

Still in the light, I propped myself up on my elbow and watched Wayne's beautiful cock twitch and grow in the open air. A slight breeze flowed in through the open door and it was like being outside, yet we were in our room. I quickly pulled off my top and, naked, grabbed Wayne's erection and squeezed.

I have to tell you that I'm not usually the sexual aggressor in our relationship. We frequently make love in the morning, but it's usually Wayne who does the suggesting. I was so hot right then, however, that I was going to have sex with my husband, whether he was in the mood or not. Of course his cock told me that he was most certainly in the mood and I squeezed him again.

Without the usual preliminaries I climbed onto my knees and, as I started to straddle Wayne's hips, he wiggled around until when I mounted him I was facing the open door. Crouched over him, I held his cock and rubbed the tip over my flowing pussy. Strange. He hadn't kissed or touched me, yet

I was more aroused than I could ever remember being.

Wayne let me do it all my way. I continued to use his cock to rub my sopping skin, then massaged my clit with it until I was ready to come even without him inside of me. I soon remedied that by positioning the tip of his cock against my opening and dropping onto it until he filled me. Eyes closed, head thrown back, unmindful of Wayne's desires, I levered myself up and down at exactly the speed I wanted, needed.

I don't ever remember being so carried away. It was as if I were on some kind of sexual overload. The sun pooled on my breasts, heating my nipples as my hands massaged Wayne's hairy chest. My pussy was full of his thick cock and I took. Up and down, over and over. I was like some animal, possessed by needs and desires I had only touched lightly before.

Suddenly I felt Wayne's hips buck and his back arch. As if I had reached some kind of precipice, I hurled myself over the edge, my screams mingling with Wayne's deep animal roar.

I collapsed on top of my husband, completely spent.

We must have dozed for quite a while because when I awoke the sun was much higher in the sky and it no longer shone onto the bed. "Holy shit," Wayne said. "I've never seen you like that before."

"I don't think I've ever felt like that before. It was as though I was some kind of sun-worshiping goddess and the rays gave me power." I slowly focused. "I'm sorry, sweetheart. I was only thinking of me. Was it okay for you too?"

I could feel Wayne's laugh deep in his chest as I lay on top of him. "Let's just put it to the test." He wrapped his arms around me and held tight. "It's about eight o'clock and the sun's already too high in the sky to shine on the bed. I'll set the alarm for six thirty tomorrow morning and you can watch to see whether I'm satisfied. If you don't hear my bellow, that is."

As it turns out we didn't need the alarm. The warmth woke us each morning and we made love in the sunshine, with the door open, until we were more exhausted when we got home than we had been when we left. We've already made reservations at the same bungalow for next year. God, I love sunshine.

In My Dreams

In my dreams she's mine, sexy, funny, and incredibly hot. She's creative, anxious to do whatever I want, whatever we want, whenever we want, and we want lots of really wild stuff. Every few nights I create her in my mind just before I fall asleep and in my dreams we do it all. If only . . .

At first I had to decide who to pattern my dream woman after. I'm not the type to just create someone, or even use a movie star or some glamorous type. No, I wanted my dream lover to be real, or as real as I could make her. Then Maggie moved in next door. I ran into her several times in the elevator and got curious.

My upstairs neighbor, Mrs. McDonald, told me all about

her one morning soon after. "Her name's Maggie Bartlett and she's been divorced about a year. She's quiet and a bit shy, keeps to herself and minds her own business," Mrs. McDonald said. "She certainly wouldn't think of prying into anyone else's business and I respect that, Cal."

Mrs. McDonald is certainly one to respect privacy, I thought sarcastically. Anyway, Maggie started to invade my fantasies. She's not terribly pretty but there's something I sensed beneath the surface, something a little sad, but hopeful, if you know what I mean. And hungry for the kind of pleasures we could create together. You probably want to know what she looks like, although it's really not important to me. Well, she's about 5′2″ with long straight dark hair and wonderful deep brown eyes. Bottomless eyes that I could drown in. She's got a dimple in her chin and I like to imagine the matching ones on her rear cheeks. She wears very little makeup and I really like that.

Last evening, like so many before, we rode up seven floors in the elevator and neither of us said a word. I kept wanting to say, "How are you this evening?" or "How was your day?" but the words wouldn't come out. We got off the elevator and, almost simultaneously, used our respective keys to open our doors. As I turned to say "Have a nice evening," her door closed so I walked inside my apartment and started building another fantasy around her. It wasn't the first time I'd imagined what it might be like, but this time it went so much further.

In my earliest visions we just got to talking in the elevator and she invited me in for a drink. We just talked. I was witty and clever and we laughed a lot. At the end of the evening, in my dream, we kissed, her lips soft and warm. Her body was pliant, bending against me, making contact chest to knees. Then it was over.

As the weeks went on, each dream got longer, more involved, more experimental, and when I came back from my fantasy land I could almost feel her, still against me, my cock hard, pressing into her. I would hold myself, rubbing my throbbing erection, while I recaptured the final moments of my latest vision. The end result was the obvious.

Tonight's illusion was the most intricate, the most erotically detailed.

As always, after a trip up in the elevator during which I am charming, engaging in bouts of clever repartee, she invites me into her apartment for a drink. She is dressed in a simple beige, cable-knit sweater and slacks, with flat black shoes. As she closes the door behind me, I look around her living room. Plants hang on long chains suspended from heavy hooks bolted into the ceiling. As I stare at those hooks, I realize that she is gazing at me. "You understand," she whispers. It's not a question. She knows.

"Yes," I say, barely able to breathe. "May we do it all?"

In my dreams there's no need for lengthy explanations. We both know everything as if we can read each other's mind.

"Yes," she sighs. "Oh, yes." She walks into the circle of my arms and I kiss her lightly. Somehow kisses aren't relevant right now.

I grab the bottom of her sweater and in one swift motion pull it off over her head. Her body is hot to my touch, her skin smooth. Her eyes are wide, her pupils dilated in expectation. I stand back and gaze at her tiny lacy bra. She slips her shoes off and reaches for the waistband of her slacks, looking at me for agreement. I nod slightly and she unbuttons her pants and lets them fall, to pool around her slender bare feet. Her panties match her bra, tiny, with lace covering the dark triangle at the apex of her thighs.

Meekly she extends her wrists. In the dream I know where everything is so I open a drawer in a bookcase and pull out two leather and Velcro straps. I fasten them to her wrists, then lift plants from two of the chains. Quickly her wrists are fastened to the hooks at the end of the chains, her arms wide, extended slightly toward the ceiling. Her eyes close in ecstasy and I watch her breathing quicken. "Yes," she whispers.

In the drawer I find a two-foot spreader bar and fasten her ankles to the sides, widening her stance. She's open, available to me, yet I know she's not uncomfortable.

I touch the crotch of her panties and she's soaked, aroused and anxious for whatever comes next. In the drawer I find a dildo. It's not a monster, just large enough to fill her pussy and keep her hot, on the edge yet not over it. I draw aside the drenched panties and easily slide the plastic cock into her. Then I replace the panties, using them to hold the dildo in place. Then I stand back and watch her hips writhe, trying to get the ultimate stimulation. "Not yet," I say.

"Please," she moans.

"When we're both ready." I fondle myself through my jeans. "When we're both ready."

She stares hungrily at my hand. "Of course."

I want her nipples, so I pull down the cups of her bra. Her tits are small, but her nubs are tight, erect and reaching for my mouth. I suck one and roll the other between my thumb and forefinger. God, she feels wonderful as she presses herself more tightly against my mouth.

I suck first one then the other, wetting her skin, running my fingernails down her back. She's going crazy, needing what only I can give her now. I reach down and find her erect clit. I stroke it but when I think she's about to come, I stop. "Not yet." This will last a long time so I press hard on her clit until she calms.

In the drawer I find nipple clamps. More stimulation. I cut her bra and it falls to the floor. I fasten the clips to her erect nipples, then tug gently on the chain connecting them. "Oh, God," she moans. "So high . . ."

"Oh yes," I say, "just a little more." I know my pleasure will be total, but I want that for her too. Only one more step.

I find an anal dildo in the drawer and apply lots of lubri-cant. Then I pull her panties aside and spread lots of lube on her ass. It takes little pressure for the dildo to slip inside, fill-ing her anus. I tap, first on the vaginal dildo, then on the anal one, causing her to scream and writhe. "Oh, please. No more," she cries, almost incoherent in her pleasure. Finally I'm sure she's ready so I unhook her wrists, remove the spreader and lower her to the soft, carpeted floor.

I drag her panties off, remove the dildo from her pussy, and ram my engorged cock home. I tug on the nipple chain and move the anal dildo so I can feel it on my cock. It takes only a moment until we both come, screaming.

I came to in my bedroom panting, my cock spurting all over my hand, my body trembling. I could almost see her, touch her, but she wasn't there.

The following evening, as we rode in the elevator together, I finally said, "Hi. My name's Cal."

"Mine's Maggie. We're neighbors."

"I know. My apartment's right next to yours."

She smiled, then started to laugh. "Of course we both know that. I've been noticing you. Would you like to stop in before dinner for a glass of wine or a beer?"

I was flabbergasted. We were talking. I was going to spend time with her. "That would be nice."

She opened her apartment door and ushered me inside. The living room was very sparsely furnished but there were several plants hanging from chains of varied lengths. When she saw me looking at the chains, she blushed. "I really like plants," she whispered, "and other things."

Woodworking Wizard

Mitch and I are probably the luckiest people on earth. We took the two things we enjoy most, woodworking and sex, and combined them into a thriving business. We make, demonstrate, and sell sex toys. Let me tell you how this all began.

One evening several years ago, Mitch, who had had a full wood shop set up in our basement for many years, arrived in the bedroom with his hands behind his back. I was sitting on the bed watching television and working on a new needlepoint. "I made something for you as a joke," he said, his hands remaining behind him.

Over the past few years, Mitch had made me some beautiful wooden jewelry, several bangle bracelets, necklaces, and earring sets. What now?, I wondered, ready to be surprised and delighted. When he remained standing in the doorway, I said, "Aren't you going to show me?"

"Actually, not just yet." He put a package wrapped in newspaper on the dresser and scurried downstairs, returning quickly with a bottle of wine and two glasses. He poured and we drank and talked, then ended up doing what we usually do. He stretched out on the bed beside me and kissed me, his lips dancing over mine, his hands caressing my hip and ribs. God, I love his hands. I closed my eyes and ran my fingers over his shirtfront, unbuttoning and caressing the skin beneath. He pulled my sweatshirt over my head and unhooked my bra, fondling my tits until I ached for him.

Let me tell you that my tits are my weakness. I love to have them sucked and pinched. "Make it hurt a little," I begged and he tweaked my nipples hard just the way I like it. As Mitch pulled my jeans and panties off, I could feel the slithery wetness between my legs. My cunt was hot and juicy and ready for Mitch's big cock. "Do me baby," I cried.

"Oh yes," he growled, "but not the way you think." He slapped me hard across one butt-cheek, then got off the bed and retrieved the package from the bureau. "This is for you," he said. "Open it now."

"Now?" I whined. I didn't want to bother with jewelry. I wanted cock. I looked into Mitch's eyes and saw that he would not be refused so I sat up and reached for the gift. I tore off the paper and saw what my fingers had felt. It was a smooth, highly polished wooden dildo, larger than Mitch's cock, or any other I had seen over the years. My eyes widened and my mouth formed a large "O."

Mitch took the dildo by the shaft and ran the tip around my startled lips. It was so smooth, almost soft, and cool against my mouth. Instinctively, I licked the swollen end. "I patterned it after my own cock," Mitch said as I licked, "but I increased the thickness by twenty percent. This ought to fill that hot pussy of yours really well. Take it, baby," he said, jamming the dildo into my sopping pussy.

Mitch fucked my pussy with the dildo, rhythmically ramming it into me and pulling it back. It was like being fucked by a big, cool cock and my cunt had never been so full. I trembled, threw my head back, and screamed. That devilishly big wooden cock in my cunt drove me to a shattering orgasm.

Mitch pulled the dildo from my body, then quickly stripped and drove his own super-hard cock into me. Momentarily I was afraid his prick wouldn't feel as good since it wasn't as big as the wooden one, but my fears were groundless. His cock felt wonderfully different and quickly brought me to another quaking orgasm. He followed almost immediately.

Later, when I had calmed, I said, "Whatever possessed you to make that?"

Mitch laughed. "You're not complaining, are you?"

"Not in the least. Just wondering where you got such a sensational idea."

"Actually, I saw an ad in a magazine for something like this and I realized that I had been wasting my time making doodads. This is much more fun. And I have a few other ideas as well."

"I couldn't wait."

Woodworking Wizard: The Paddle

My husband Mitch, the woodworking wizard, had been very secretive for several weeks. Finally one evening he arrived in the bedroom with his next surprise. It was after ten and I was undressing for bed. Standing in a shortie nightgown, I gazed at him as his shoulders filled the doorway. "I have made something I know you'll enjoy," he said, taking his hands from behind his back. His large hands held a paddle, a bit larger than a ping-pong paddle, with a longer handle and a textured surface rather like a fancy carving board.

"W-w-what's that for?" I asked, knowing full well exactly what he had in mind. I had always been turned-on by a little pain during our lovemaking, but we had never tried anything like the instrument he was holding. On occasion Mitch had slapped my bottom just as I was about to climax and that smack seemed to enhance my orgasm but this was something much more. Was I ready for something so much more serious?

"You know exactly what I'm thinking," he said, "so let's not kid each other. You've been a very naughty girl recently and you need a few whacks with this little beauty."

He slapped the paddle against his palm and my knees began to shake. Did I really want this? Did he understand things about me that I didn't? Was he right? The wetness between my thighs said yes; he knows me only too well.

A small smile curved my husband's mouth. "I can see from the look in your eyes, that you understand and that I'm right." I stared at his long slender fingers as they caressed the highly polished mahogany. "Just a quick rule. Say, 'Marshmallow.'"

"Marshmallow."

Mitch put the paddle on the bed and stared at me, a serious expression on his face. "If anything I do causes you more pain than you want, even a tiny bit, you have to say Marshmallow. I'll stop, immediately. I promise. Please, you have to agree to say the magic word. If you don't, I won't know whether I'm doing something to really hurt you."

"Did you figure out this magic word thing?"

"Actually I've done a lot of reading about spanking and pain and this is the only way to play safely. It's important."

"Okay," I said, "but why can't I just say 'stop'."

"You might want to yell at me to stop and not really mean it. In the stories I've read, many people being lightly paddled enjoy begging for their lover to stop, but they don't really mean it."

I nodded. "Sounds sensible."

Mitch reached for the paddle and slowly, almost sensuously picked it up from the bed. "Good. Now let's talk about your punishment."

My knees were shaking and I dropped onto the edge of the bed. "Punishment?" I couldn't take my eyes from his hands caressing the surface of the wooden paddle.

"I thought maybe five."

I tried to speak, then swallowed and cleared my throat. "Five?"

"Just five for starters." He sat beside me on the edge of the bed and patted his lap. "I'm sure you can figure out the proper position."

As I slowly climbed over his lap, I thought about the thin layer of nylon that would be all that protected my bottom. I took a deep breath. Marshmallow. I could always call things off, but the thought of everything I was about to experience made my knees tremble with excitement.

I settled across Mitch's lap. "You know," he said, "you have a really nice bottom and those tiny panties are really sexy. However, I think your bottom needs to be naked." He pulled the back of the panties down so my cheeks were totally exposed. Then he rubbed the cool paddle over my heated skin.

He chuckled. "You're trembling." He raised the paddle and brought it down on my skin, hard enough to make a loud smack, but not hard enough to cause anything but a mild sting. Then he reached between my thighs and rubbed my pussy. "And this is making you really sopping."

I wanted to deny the pleasure of the paddle, but why? I was enjoying something kinky with my husband. Another swat and a bit more sting. A third and a fourth. I had lost track of exactly where his hands were and what they were doing. He alternately caressed my ass-cheeks, rubbed my pussy, and swatted my bottom.

"One more for my naughty girl," he purred, and he brought the paddle down harder for the last swat. Then he rubbed my clit and, with little warning, I came. "Oh shit!" I screamed. "Yes, baby. Once more. Do it again."

I could hear him chuckle again, then the paddle hit my bottom hard, creating an ecstatic punctuation to my orgasm. "Yes!"

"Darling, that was so good," Mitch said, softly caressing my cheeks.

"Fantastic," I panted.

"And now that you've been punished, will you promise to be a good girl from now on?"

I climbed off my husband's lap and grinned at him. "Not on your life."

The Woman Who Tried to Seduce Death

Excerpts from the field journals of Susan Talbot, extraterrestrial ethnomythologist.

I'm an ethnomythologist. Loosely translated that means that I collect stories, fables from some of the hundreds of new humanoid cultures that space exploration has encountered. At the beginning myths weren't considered important, but as we tried to relate to new culture after new culture it became obvious that to understand a people it is necessary to understand their mythology, and that's the guiding principle behind my work. Thus ethnomythologists became an important adjunct to every exploration team.

In my travels to multiple worlds collecting myths and fables, the stories created by the sexually active and uninhibited people of Sh'a'i are among the most interesting to me. This one concerns a woman who tried to cheat death.

In olden times, G'ef, the god of heaven and hell, came to pick up his victims in person. Just before the moment of death, G'ef would appear to personally conduct his chosen one to either the underworld or heaven. It was a woman named Pr'ai'a who ended this practice.

One afternoon, Pr'ai'a was sitting in her garden, weaving a small basket out of grasses, when a handsome man appeared before her. "Good afternoon, sir," she said, a bit startled at having such a beautiful man just materialize in front of her.

"Good afternoon to you. Do you know who I am?" he said, his voice liquid and alluring.

"No, sir, I do not," she said, continuing to wet the grasses and weave the intricate patterns she made so well.

"I am G'ef. I've come for you."

Pr'ai'a was horrified. She had lived only nineteen summers and, although she had several wonderful lovers, she hadn't had any children yet. She wasn't ready to go, even to T'a'i, their heaven. "But . . ."

"I'm afraid there aren't any buts, my dear. I'm here for you."

"Does it have to be right now? Can't you wait a few turns?"

"I'm sorry," G'ef said. "I've come for you."

"Maybe you can wait just a few minutes," Pr'ai'a said. "I can make you a cup of delicious Wa'a tea. No one else makes it as well as I do."

"We really should leave now," G'ef said, "in case I get another call. I have to hurry so I can finish one job before the gods send me my next one, you know."

Pr'ai'a smiled her most charming smile. "I make the best Wa'a tea in the village. And you haven't gotten another message yet, have you?"

"No, I haven't. And I do like Wa'a tea. Maybe just a cup. But if the gods call for me to conduct someone else then we'll have to hurry. They don't like to be kept waiting."

Pr'ai'a nodded as she walked quickly into her house and put some water over the fire to boil. As she waited, she thought about Mr. Death. He had his orders but if she delayed him, maybe, just maybe, the gods might be angry with him and intervene. Maybe if he didn't take her in time, she'd be spared. She thought she could delay him for a short while and that might be enough.

She rummaged through her belongings and found a small pouch of a special herb the medicine woman had given her several moons before. Yes, she thought, this just might do the trick. She sprinkled just a pinch of the herb into the cup and covered it with the leaves of the Wa'a plant. Then she paused, and added another pinch of the herb. As she filled the cup with boiling water her hands shook. Everything depended on the next few minutes.

She put the cup on a tray and, steadying her hands, carried the tray back into her garden. Placing it on a small table she lifted the cup and handed it to G'ef. "I made it especially for you."

"Aren't you going to have any?" he asked, taking the cup.

"I just had some a little while ago," she said, "and I'd like to write a letter to my mother before we go."

G'ef sipped the tea. "This is wonderful," he said, "but if you want to write a note, do it quickly. We really have to leave."

Pr'ai'a found a small piece of skin and quickly began a note to her mother. As she wrote, she watched G'ef out of the corner of her eye as he sipped his tea. "It's very warm in the garden today," he said after a few minutes. "Do you mind if I remove my Ra'm?"

"Of course not," Pr'ai'a said. "In fact, you're right. It is warm. I'll remove mine too." She stood and slowly unwound the long cloth that was The Peoples' only garment. Slowly she let it drop to the ground, letting G'ef see how wonderfully formed her body was, hoping the herb was working. As he stood to remove his Ra'm she saw that his penis was growing hard. She knelt at his feet, picked up his cloth, and folded it neatly.

"Is that better?" she asked.

"Not really," he said. "I still feel very warm all over."

"That's too bad," Pr'ai'a said. "Let me get a cold cloth and cool you down. I have one right here that I was using to soften the reeds for my weaving." She got the small cloth and began to wash G'ef's heated body. She poured a small amount of water over his shoulders and sponged his back and buttocks. "You're body is finely formed," she purred. "Turn around now."

When he turned, she wiped the cool cloth over his hairless chest and down his flanks. "Is this helping?" she asked, seemingly innocently.

"No. Not at all," G'ef groaned.

"Maybe this will," she said, wetting her lush body and rubbing her breasts and belly against his. "Does this feel nice?"

"Yes," he moaned. "Oh yes."

She parted her thighs and pressed his now-rampant penis against her heated sex. "And this?"

"Yes," he said, now barely able to stand.

"Sit here," she said, indicating the chair she had been sitting on, and he dropped into it. "Now, let me sit on your lap and use my cloth to try to cool you." She dipped the cloth into the cool water, then straddled his lap, her breasts only inches from his mouth. She stroked the cloth over his arms, brushing her nipples against his lips. Soon his mouth opened and she felt the pulling as he suckled. "Yes," she purred. "That's right."

He seemed unable to resist her and she felt the familiar stirring between her legs. She knew she was getting aroused from the sucking on her nipples and she wanted her passage filled, but she had to go slowly, delay as long as she could. She cupped one breast and fed it into his eager mouth, feeling the juices fill her passage and slowly trickle down her spread thighs.

G'ef's hands were on her now and she felt him squeezing and kneading her buttocks. As he sucked, he began to move his hips, thrusting against her mound. There was a sudden gust of wind but it didn't cool either of them. Slowly he lifted her then lowered her onto his staff. Smiling, she felt his shaft fill her, sliding deep into her hot, wet passage. G'ef held her bottom and raised and lowered her on his manhood, pounding into her, bucking and panting, making growling sounds.

Again she felt a strong gust of wind, but she continued to lever herself on him as he sucked on her nipples. Suddenly, with a great roar, he spilled himself into her. She clenched her inner muscles and held him until she felt the familiar spasms of her own pleasure. Finally spent, the two quieted.

"What happened?" G'ef asked.

A roar from the heavens answered, "You totally forgot your job, that's what happened. I called you twice."

"Oh J'al, I'm sorry. She must have tricked me." He picked up his Ra'm and quickly covered his naked body. "I don't know what came over me."

The god's voice softened. "This lovely, devious woman overcame you in every sense of the word. She distracted you so thoroughly that you failed to hear the calling. Woman," the voice said to Pr'ai'a, "you have done what no other woman has ever done. I can't decide whether you should be punished for your audacity or rewarded."

With a soft breeze, a woman's voice interrupted. "Don't you dare punish her. She's done something magical. She's seduced Death." Her laugh filled the sky. "How delightful. He always was something of a prude."

"You're right, A'wa," the male voice boomed. "Pr'ai'a, you shall live for many more summers and bear many children. And as for G'ef, well, we will have a long talk about these personal visits of yours." And with that, G'ef disappeared and the sky quieted.

Pr'ai'a grinned. She had tricked death, and had enjoyed every moment of it. Yet, she was still feeling very warm. Maybe one of her lovers was nearby to help her. She'd have to wander around the village and see. She picked up what remained of the cup of tea and started toward the village.

From then on, when it was time for death to take any of The People, he took no chances. He now does his work invisibly and silently.

Ki'otro

Excerpts from the field journals of Susan Talbot, extraterrestrial ethnomythologist.

As with so many cultures I've studied, the people of Sh'a'i have a superhero character, sort of a combination of Superman and the Lone Ranger from old-time earth. On Sh'a'i it's Ki'otro, an ordinary man with extraordinary abilities. It is said he can change the course of rivers to help the crops or prevent a flood, kill invaders that threaten a village, scoop water from the sea to stop a fire, or save a village from wild beasts.

Ki'otro is said to be taller than the average Sh'a'i man, with a handsome face and long straight blond hair that he wears in the traditional three braids. He wears only a small loincloth over the well-developed muscles and smooth skin of his handsome body.

There are hundreds of tales of his exploits and, as with everything else on Sh'a'i, many of the stories tell of his sexual prowess. For example:

One difficult cold moon season, food was scarce. All The People were hungry, as were the many beasts of the forest. There came a day when a pack of wild G'ama made their way from the high mountain, through the woods, toward a remote village, hoping for an easy meal. The villagers heard the ugly sound the beasts made and shut their children away in their houses. For several turns, the beasts could be heard, snuffling and growling, looking for food.

It was said that one unfortunate family left their door unlatched when they went to the edge of the forest to try to find enough berries and seeds to make an evening repast. Their three small children discovered the unfastened door and wandered outside, happy to be freed from their captivity. They ran and whooped and chased each other around the house, working off their youthful energy. Soon they attracted the attention of the beasts who slunk toward them through the undergrowth.

The children's parents heard the commotion and ran back to the house, only to find a dozen wild beasts slinking toward their children. "No!" they screamed. "Get away, you beasts!" They ran, waving their arms, trying to frighten the animals away. It was no use. The beasts had smelled the odor of the children and knew that they would fill many empty bellies. "Help!" the parents cried. "Help our children."

Suddenly from the forest came a crashing and thrashing and the thudding of running feet. It was Ki'otro, pounding through the scrub. He emerged from the shadows of the trees, grabbed one beast in each hand and threw them into a far field. Two more suffered the same fate. Several more were punched and kicked until the entire pack slunk off into the woods to lick their wounds.

"We can't thank you enough," the parents said to Ki'otro, after several minutes of hugging and yelling at their children.

"What made the beasts so brave? Usually they stay far away from people."

"They are hungry, as are we all. It's been a very bad cold moon season and food is scarce."

"I can fix that," Ki'otro said. He disappeared into the forest, and returned the following day with two foodbeasts, one slung over each shoulder. The animals were already cleaned and ready for the cooking pot. On his back he had a large bag of leafy plants and root vegetables and around his waist he wore a small pack filled with succulent herbs. He piled all the food in the center of the village as the entire population gathered around. "This should hold you until the first warm moon," Ki'otro said, "but if you have any more trouble, just ring the town bell and I'll come and help you again."

"How can we thank you?" the elders asked.

"Let me come to the New Earth Festival, in the warm moon season when the crops are growing and things are more plentiful. Let me choose from among your women for company for the night."

Several of the women stared and trembled with desire, others sighed just to think of spending the night with Ki'otro. He was the handsomest, most virile, sexiest man they had ever seen. Other women giggled. What an honor it would be, they thought. "Of course," the elders said. "We will sound the drums to summon you and you will be most welcome, the guest of honor. All the women will dance and you can choose as many as you like." Everyone knew that Ki'otro wouldn't be satisfied with just one.

Thankfully the cold moon season ended early that rotation and soon the grass became green, the foodbeasts returned from their faraway feeding grounds, and the grain grew tall in the fields. The New Earth Festival was planned to last for three turns, with games and contests, singing and dancing, and, most of all, lots of food and wine. The word was sent throughout the area that all were welcome, including, and most importantly, Ki'otro.

On the evening of the festival's first turn, seven massive drums pounded out their visceral rhythms, calling all to the event. The beat echoed through every person, making bodies sway and hearts emulate the meter. Faster and faster the drums sounded until the entire center of the village was filled with

swaying men and women. Then, abruptly, the drums were
silent. All the people stilled. Into the center of the mass of villagers strode Ki'otro. His body shone with a mixture of precious oils and herbs, making his muscular form almost glow in
the firelight. Black leather thongs were tied around his biceps,
guiding all the women's eyes to his mighty shoulders and arms.
He wore his long blond hair in three braids, tied with matching thongs. The cloth that girdled his loins was the softest tan
and molded itself to his massive hips. On his feet were sandals,
cross-laced up his calves.

Older women sighed as he passed, knowing he would never
choose them for his entertainment. Younger women attempt-
ed to catch his eye. Pick me, they prayed. Some even stepped
in front of him to try to get his attention but he walked to
where the council of elders gathered without looking left or
right.

"Ki'otro," the elders said. "You honor us with your pres-
ence." One older man handed him a cup of wine, another
gave him a joint of foodbeast. Still another elder pulled a
soft leather ground cover toward him and urged him to seat
himself so the women could dance. For hours the women
danced while Ki'otro watched as he ate and drank and
shared stories with the elders. Finally, as the fires burned
low, the elders asked him whether he was ready to choose.
"Knowing of your visit many of the young women have been
keeping themselves from the village men so they would still

be untouched when you came," the chief of the village explained. "Any of our women would be proud to share your company tonight."

"Thank you," Ki'otro said. He looked around the large group, catching the eye of several of the maidens. "I know that whoever is chosen will be glad to share my bed. I also know that those who aren't chosen will be unhappy, and it's difficult for me to make anyone sad." He again gazed at the women, most now naked in the flickering light. He paused and, except for the crackling of the fire, the silence was complete. "In the time since I saved your children from the beasts I have learned a lot about your people. Therefore, I will choose three widows. Pri, Cavan, and La'i."

The crowd gasped. "But they are all old. La'i has nearly thirty winters. Cavan has birthed four children. Pri has out-lived three husbands." Ki'otro looked over at where the three widows were sitting together, surprise and delight written all over their faces.

"I know all this. I also know that their husbands were all happy with their wives and told many of how creative they were in lovemaking." When the buzzing in the village grew louder, Ki'otro signaled for silence. "I know some of you women have kept yourself for me but I find I don't want untried women who do not yet know the art of pleasuring. Women of the village, learn from your men; and men, learn from your women. Learn the value of experience, too." He stretched out his hand and guided the three selected women to their feet. He draped his arms around their shoulders and together they walked toward the tent they were to share.

Pri smiled and rubbed her hand over Ki'otro's massive chest. "You are as wise as you are brave," she purred. "I know my friends and I can give you much pleasure." Ki'otro threw back the skin that covered the opening of the tent and the four stepped inside. Quickly Ki'otro built a fire and soon the tent was filled with warmth and dancing lights. Cavan went to one side of the tent and opened a small pouch of herbs. She took a small handful and threw it on the fire. Soon a pleasant scent filled the tent and began to loosen their remaining inhibitions. "My body isn't as beautiful as many others," La'i said, slowly removing her covering cloth.

Ki'otro gazed at her. "It's not how beautiful you are, but how clever you are at i'i that I want." He looked at the other two. "And you as well." He stretched out on the soft fur covering the floor and held out his arms. "Come here."

The other two women unwound their cloths and the three gathered around Ki'otro. Pri and Cavan each untied one of the thongs that bound his sandals and slowly unlaced them from his massive calves, while La'i unbraided his hair. Slowly they all touched his body, stroking his face, his legs, his feet, and hands. As Ki'otro's eyes closed, six hands caressed his skin with feather-light fingers, then with sharp nails. He found his member growing hard and strong from the sensations all over his body. He waited for one of the women to unfasten his tan loincloth. But no one did.

When it was obvious to the women that he was becoming impatient, Pri purred, "It is best when it is savored. Let us show you how good it can be before i'i. We have all night and more."

For long minutes, Ki'otro lay on the fur with hands all over his body. Then he felt something pressing his palm. A breast, nipple fully erect. He slowly closed his fingers and kneaded the soft flesh. Another breast in the other hand, full and warm. As he played with his treasures, a piece of fur was being stroked up and down his thighs and tiny bites were being placed on his shoulders. He had no idea which woman was where, and somehow it added to his intoxication.

Then someone whispered, "Open your mouth." When he did, one of the breasts left his fingers and pressed against his lips. He sucked, licked, and bit the succulent flesh while he felt the cloth being untied from around his waist. He wanted to tell the women what his member wanted, but his mouth was so beautifully occupied. Lips pressed tiny kisses on his staff, causing fluid to leak from the tip. Fingers stroked his pouch and scratched the tender area behind. When he thought he would explode, fingers encircled the base of his staff and closed tightly so he couldn't climax.

Lips kissed the tip of his staff. A soft tongue licked, then a mouth closed over him. He felt the breast in his hand lift and a wet slit rub over his fingers. It was hard to concentrate. He wanted to stroke the sopping folds and suck the tit and feel the magic the mouth was working on his member but it was difficult to keep focused.

A hand guided his fingers into the wet channel, filling it until he could feel pulses begin. The breast left his mouth and another wet slit covered his mouth. He pushed his tongue into the opening then felt another channel cover his staff. Three wet women, one on his hand, one in his mouth, and one covering his member. It was too wonderful. With a buck of his hips, he filled one with his juices. He completed one woman with his mouth and one with his hand, then collapsed into sleep, arms filled with naked flesh.

Food was brought in several times each day for the remaining days of the festival so that the four didn't have to leave the tent. At the end of the third day, they emerged, smiling and exhausted. "Was the reward enough to thank you for all you've done for us?" the leader of the elders asked, still puzzled by Ki'otro's selection.

Ki'otro smiled and hugged and kissed the three women to the cheers of the villagers. "It was more than I could ever have wanted. I thank you."

As he walked back toward the forest, several of the younger women came over to Pri, Cavan, and La'i. Shyly, one said,

"Was he wonderful?" When the three just grinned, another asked, "Could you teach us about pleasuring?"

"Of course," Cavan said. "We are all sisters and i'i is the best thing there is. We will teach you and you can teach the men." Pri winked. "Actually," she added, "we can teach the men too."

The Valley of Entwined Lovers

Excerpts from the field journals of Susan Talbot,
extraterrestrial ethnomythologist.

In my travels to multiple worlds collecting myths and fables, the stories created by the incredibly sexually active and uninhibited people of Sh'a'i are among the most interesting to me. This one concerns a group of unusual rock formations. Scientists say that when lava from a volcanic eruption flowed over the indigenous paired-trees of the Ba'lan plain, they produced what look like statues of entwined lovers. The People tell a different story.

As far back as The People can remember there have been festivals. In Sh'a'i life was easy, with ample food that the men of the village could easily hunt from the herds of wild animals, fish from the many lakes and rivers, grains and vegetables from the fields that The People farmed, fruits and berries from the trees and bushes that surrounded the village. So The People flourished and enjoyed life.

They particularly enjoyed parties, the bigger the better, and the village elders spent much time planning the many festivals that dotted The Peoples' calendar. The People particularly enjoyed the festival of B'a'at, the god of the wine. Every rotation, they harvested the fruits they used to make the wine, and, as they crushed the small round red berries, they drank the wine that had been made the previous year.

One rotation, the wine was particularly strong and the people became particularly merry. There was dancing and slowly, all thoughts turned to i'i. Ani, a beautiful woman of nineteen rotations, danced to attract the eye of Cara'i, a handsome young man she'd had her eye on for many moons. She wore her winding cloth so that it covered her full breasts and most of her body. As she danced near Cara'i she moved so that one long leg teasingly showed between the layers of cloth. She had placed tiny manto nuts on a string around one ankle and one wrist so that as she danced the dry seeds inside made an enticing clicking. Cara'i noticed and began to watch Ani as she moved sensuously in front of him.

Slowly, Ani allowed the upper part of her winding cloth to slip from one shoulder, allowing one full breast to peek out, showing Cara'i the erect nipple. Grinning, Cara'i stood up and joined in the dance, first moving close, then slipping away, his body glowing in the firelight. Other dancers separated and slowly stopped dancing to watch the couple as they teased. Cara'i danced close and when his body was almost touching Ani's he moved his loincloth aside so that his erect penis could rub against her hip. When she reached for it, he snapped the cloth over his erection and danced away. A few moments later, Ani pressed her body against Cara'i's, moving against him sensuously, like a beast in heat. She stood behind him and opened her winding cloth, then pressed her naked breasts against his back.

Her body never lost contact with his skin as she crouched down and rubbed her breasts the length of his buttocks and thighs. The people watching clapped in rhythm with the drums, urging the couple on. Ani needed no urging. She freed her long yellow hair from its binding and used it to brush against Cara'i's back. Then she danced around to his chest, rotating her head so that her hair washed against his damp, heated skin.

As she danced, she could feel the sweat trickling down her body, mingling with the fluids that gathered between her legs. She looked at the front of Cara'i's loincloth and saw the obvious evidence of his enjoyment of the dance. Her nipples were tight, the peaks yearning for his fingers and his mouth.

Slowly she unwound her outer winding cloth so that her

breasts fell free, swaying with her movements. When he next danced close, she took his hands and placed them against her crests, filling his palms with her heated flesh. She melded her movements to his so that they were rhythmically swaying with the drum beats. She let her head fall backward, her eyes closed.

"No," Cara'i said. "Open your eyes. Watch my hands as they pleasure your breasts."

Ani opened her eyes and gazed at Cara'i. As they turned, she could see that their dance was exciting their audience. While all the villagers watched them, they also touched each other, stroking and sucking. The sight of mouths on penises, legs spread, hands never still, pushed the two dancers to an even higher pitch. Someone handed Ani a cup of wine and she took a long drink. Then she tipped the cup so that some of the deep red liquid trickled down her chest and formed droplets that hung from her nipples. She cupped her breasts in her palms and, as she moved, Ani offered the almond crests to Cara'i.

He didn't resist the offer. His hips bucking in imitation of mating, he moved closer, then bent and licked the ruby drops from Ani's breasts. Moving together he suckled, shafts of delight rocking her body, shooting pleasures through her belly to that special place between her legs.

Finally he stood straight and lifted Ani's chin so she could again gaze into his eyes. She placed her palms on his slippery shoulders, her hands gliding down his muscular upper arms, then to his smooth chest. As he reached down to remove her inner cloth, she pulled at the knot and released his loincloth. Quickly the two were naked, dancing in all their glory while the other villagers drank, and sucked, and coupled on the grass.

Cara'i grabbed a flower from a table and brushed the soft, fragrant petals over Ani's breasts. Then he slowly slid the flower down her belly until, as she parted her thighs, it caressed her sex. Over and over the velvety petals stroked until her body was pounding with need. Then Cara'i picked her up, wrapped her legs around his waist, and, never missing a beat of the drums, thrust his penis into her feverish body.

She felt filled as she had never felt filled before and, as Cara'i sucked one crest into his mouth and nipped at the tip, she felt the spasms of her climax rock her. Her inner muscles pulled his seed from him and, with a great movement of his hips, he came deep inside of her.

Mostly the gods were enjoying the spectacle of Ani and Cara'i's dance and the villagers all making i'i around them. The god R'ogg, however, was angry. "It's not decent," he raged. "All that i'i. Will the people be ready to farm the fields and hunt tomorrow? This festival has gotten to be too much."

"R'ogg is in one of his moods again," one of the lesser gods said. "He's such a prude."

"Leave them alone, R'ogg," another said. "They are having

a wonderful time and harming no one. Stop being such a spoil-sport."

R'ogg glared at the other gods. "You allow this. You even encourage it. You taught them to make wine. It's disgusting." He extended his hands in front of him, lightning shooting from his fingertips.

"What are you doing?" someone cried.

"I'm going to turn them all to stone." Lightning filled the sky over the lovers and, in an instant, every entwined couple was turned to stone. R'ogg stalked off.

Once R'ogg was out of hearing range, Qaa, a low-ranking god, began to laugh. "What are you laughing about?" several gods asked.

"Don't you see what he just did? Those lovers will now be making i'i for all eternity, and as new People are born, they will see the entwined lovers and what pleasure they were having."

And the rock-hardened paired lovers remain to this day. And at almost every moon new lovers make i'i in the field where the statues play, trying to enjoy their loving as much as the stone lovers do.

Doma

Excerpts from the field journals of Susan Talbot,
extraterrestrial ethnomythologist.

Thousands of years ago, the people of Sh'a'i dwelled in small villages, living a simple life, enjoying each other in the way the Gods ordained. The evenings were warm, life easy, and they engaged in i'i as often as they could without regard to permanent partnership until children were born. Life was peaceful and the population multiplied.

In a small village lived a teenaged girl named Doma. Doma had always been a sickly child and for all her seasons she had been too weak to participate in any of the activities that the young people of Sh'a'i normally engaged in. Although she had spent her school time in her parents' hut in her remote village, sitting quietly and avoiding any

stress on her weakened body, her mother taught her everything she needed to know. Thus she knew how to cook, she
knew how to keep house, how to weave, and how to stitch.
Over the years she had also learned all the old legends and
stories.

The only part of her education that was lacking was the art
of loving. Since sexual activities were encouraged and thoroughly enjoyed by adults and teens alike, the young people of
Sh'a'i learned of lovemaking early. After fifteen winters there
was a sexual coming-of-age ceremony that involved initiating
young men and women alike into the joys of erotic activities.
Sadly, Doma hadn't been strong enough to attend the coming-
of-age ceremony as it was feared that the pounding pulse and
rapid breathing of sexual activities would severely damage her
already weakened system. Doma, at almost nineteen, was still
almost completely ignorant and the villagers thought it was
best to keep her that way.

One afternoon, Bra'a, Doma's mother, hurried into their
hut and told Doma that a giant ship from far across the great
sea had sailed into the small harbor. "A dozen men got off,
tired and hungry. They told us that they had been lost at sea
for several weeks." Bra'a panted and took a few sips of water.
"One of them is a great healer who was traveling to the great
city. While he was eating I told him about you. I described
your sickness and he's agreed to see you and try to make you
well again. He thinks he can do it." Her mother grabbed

Doma's shoulders and stared into her deep brown eyes. "Do you know what that means? You can get well!"

Doma couldn't quite catch her breath. "Do you really think he can cure me?"

Moments later a heavy-set man with a long black beard and sparkling blue eyes entered the hut. "Good afternoon," he said, his voice soft and filled with caring. Over the next hour the doctor asked Doma dozens of questions, listened to her breathing and heart, then tested the strength in her arms and legs. Finally, he said, "Much of her problem is due to her forced inactivity. She needs to go out in the sun, be with people, get exercise. The rest we can fix with herbs and a powder I have aboard our ship. I can guarantee that if she does what I tell her to do for several weeks, she'll be as healthy as any woman in the village."

And it was true. At the end of several turns Doma was able to walk down to the stream and help her mother wash clothes. She pounded roots into flour and helped gather the local fruits and vegetables that made up much of the villager's diet. For the first time since her birth, she felt completely healthy.

She was anxious to learn about the joys of lovemaking, but since she was plain-featured and uneducated, the young men of the village wanted nothing to do with her. They were accustomed to women who knew how to pleasure men, not untrained know-nothings. They didn't want to teach, only to enjoy.

One evening, as she helped bank the communal cooking fire, she overheard a girl and boy of about her age giggling about the lovemaking they were looking forward to when it would become full dark. Doma stood and walked slowly to the beach toward a small cove she had recently discovered. She knew it would be a quiet spot where she could think.

What was she to do? she wondered as she settled herself on a rock, dangling her feet in the warm water. She knew nothing about loving, and with no one to teach her, she never would. As tears slowly trickled down her cheeks, she said, aloud, "What am I to do?"

Suddenly a man appeared, walking in the shallow sea. "Let me help you," he said.

"Who are you?" she asked, totally puzzled. He had just appeared. He hadn't walked from the beach; she would have seen him. He hadn't come from the sea, his loincloth was dry.

She couldn't stop looking at him. His face was handsome, more beautiful than any man from the village, with deep brown eyes and long brown hair worn in the traditional three braids. His body was beautifully formed, tall and lean, with wide shoulders and narrow hips. His chest was smooth, his shoulders well muscled. His legs were long with a sprinkling of dark brown hair. His hands were large, with long slender fingers. She smiled. Even his feet were beautiful as he walked across the smooth sand of the cove.

"I am F'am," he said, his voice soft, almost a whisper. "I have come to help you."

She rubbed the tears from her cheeks with the heels of her hands. "How can you help me?"

"You're such a silly child," he said. "Don't you know who I am?"

Until that moment the man's name hadn't registered in Doma's mind. Suddenly, it echoed in her brain. "F'am," she whispered, the God of loving and families. Quickly Doma covered her face with her hands to hide her embarrassment. "I'm not beautiful or smart. I'm only a plain and ignorant girl," she whispered. "Surely I'm not worthy of your time,"

"Every woman is worthy," F'am said. "Every woman is a gift from the Gods, designed for a man to enjoy, as every man is a gift for every woman." He reached out and took her hands in his.

Doma trembled as F'am touched her fingers. His hands were warm and soft, not cool and rough like the hands of the men of the village. She felt the heat of his touch warm her. "But . . . I'm so ignorant." Again unbidden, tears flowed down her cheeks.

"Little one," F'am said, "it can be a man's pleasure to teach a woman the ways of i'i." He guided her to her feet, then brushed the tears from her cheeks with the soft pad of his thumb.

F'am obviously didn't understand. "I am old," Doma said,

her voice hoarse from attempting to control her misery, "and know nothing."

"I know, and that is what has brought me here. I haven't had the joy of teaching a maiden about i'i in so many seasons. Let me show you."

Doma gazed into his eyes, her face alight with possibilities. To be taught by the God of loving. Would he? Could she? She lowered her gaze, still unable to believe. "Would you?" she said, her voice barely audible.

Her answer was a smile. Then F'am wrapped his strong arms around her and held her close. At first hesitant, Doma slowly allowed her body to relax against his, marveling in the differences between them. His chest was wide and strong, bare above his loincloth. His heartbeat comforted her as did the hardness of his torso, the strength of his arms around her. Slowly F'am released her. "You say you are plain, but every woman is a joy to behold." He loosened her hair from its thong and draped the straight, black, waist-length strands over her shoulders. "You hair is like a silken curtain." He touched her face. "You skin is like the sweetest honey, your eyes like prata."

She had never thought of her skin as being like honey, or her eyes like the strong drink The People consumed at festivals. She looked at his face to assure herself that he wasn't mocking her, and all she saw there was joy and wonder.

"Let me see all of you," F'am said, and he unfastened her winding cloth and, with a bravery she wasn't sure she understood, allowed it to fall at her feet, leaving her clad only in the tiny inner cloth that covered her mound. "Yes," he sighed, reaching out and filling his hands with her ample breasts, "so lovely." He knelt so his face was level with her chest. "Your skin is smooth, your nipples deep chocolate."

Although Doma knew that her body was nothing special, she knew that F'am was seeing it with eyes clouded from i'i. "Everyone is beautiful to someone who is interested in i'i," she said.

"That is true," he said, "and a great truth it is, Doma. Loving creates beauty and beauty is loving. In i'i everyone is beautiful." He paused, then said, "And everyone is capable of wondrous talent."

Doma wanted to argue. Being a good lover needed to be learned. As F'am's hands roamed over her breasts, however, Doma's body trembled. She was barely able to remain standing and was incapable of speaking even a single word. His thumbs rubbed her nipples until they hardened and heat flowed from them to her belly and below.

Then his mouth found her erect nipple and he suckled. Had he not been supporting her with his large hands on her back, she would have melted, collapsed into a heap on the sand of the cove. He must have known how she felt so he quickly spread her winding cloth on the sand and lay her on it. "You should see yourself in the moonlight," he purred. "So fair, your eyes hot with passion, yet puzzled since you know not what to expect. Don't fear. I'll make it as beautiful as you are."

Doma lay, shaking with need for something, yet she didn't know what it was.

When her eyes began to drift shut, F'am said, "Look at me, Doma. See what happens to a man who desires a woman such as you are." He unfastened his loincloth and dropped it on the sand. Beneath, Doma saw his staff, huge, hard, reaching from his groin.

"You are magnificent," she said, "but I don't understand."

"You will, my lovely." He stretched out on the cloth beside her and found her mouth with his. They kissed, slowly opening to each other, probing the depths of each other's mouth. She knew bliss then, and tangled her fingers in his hair to hold him close. Slowly his kisses moved down her neck and again his lips found her breasts. She could barely think, so hot were the stabs of pleasure that rocked her to her core. His mouth moved lower while his fingers unwound her inner cloth. His fingers explored her most secret place, sliding through the moisture he found there.

"You are so wet, my precious. So very ready for my staff to fill you."

Doma suddenly understood how it was going to happen, and she didn't think it was possible. "But . . ."

Then his mouth followed his fingers and she was lost. She couldn't think. She could do nothing but feel. She found her body moving without her control, reaching for him, trying to draw him closer. As his tongue probed, explored, she felt heat mounting deep in her belly, a giant wave building, becoming taller and taller. Then she felt his fingers, rubbing, stroking, and the sensation was too much. She wanted it to stop, yet she wanted it to continue forever. Higher and higher, bigger and bigger until the wave broke, cresting, overwhelming, controlling her body, clenching and unclenching with spasms of a joy so profound she wept.

Long minutes later, she opened her eyes and looked at the God/man who had shown her so much. Smiling, she reached out and slid the tips of her fingers over his smooth chest, then lower toward his rampant erection. Afraid of what she was doing, she stopped.

"Touch everything," F'am purred. "You can make me feel as wonderful as you just did."

"But I don't know how," Doma groaned.

"There's nothing to 'know.' Just do what you wish and you'll know what gives me pleasure."

"But how?"

"Look, listen, feel."

So Doma slowly slid her hands lower until she could feel the coarse hair at the root of his staff. As she touched she felt him tremble, as she had. He *was* telling her. As she found his twin sacs and held them in the palm of her hand he moaned and his staff became still larger. She wrapped the fingers of her other hand around his hardness and slid her fingers toward the base, then upward toward the tip. She felt a small drop of thick fluid flow from the end. Another way he was telling her how good it felt? "Oh yes," he moaned.

She knew what she wanted to do, yet she was hesitant. "Just do whatever you like," F'am said, his voice raspy, his breathing quick. She could feel the beat of his heart in her hands. She reached out her tongue, wet her lips, then touched the tip of her tongue to the end of his staff. It tasted different, yet pleasant, tangy like the sea.

After several minutes of exploration, F'am pressed her back against the cloth and stretched out beside her. "Now the best part," he whispered, his breath hot against her ear.

"Best part?" Doma couldn't believe anything could be more magnificent that what she had experienced so far, but she trusted F'am; so, at his touch, she spread her legs and felt him settle between them.

"There might be some pain," he warned, "but it will only be for a moment, then it will be the most amazing pleasure." He pressed the tip of his rod against her opening, then thrust inside. She was slick with her juices so his entry was quick and sure. There was a moment of pain but when Doma cried out F'am's mouth covered hers. Then the pain was gone and she felt the fullness of i'i for the first time. Again she felt the wave building as F'am's body withdrew, then entered, over and over, faster and faster.

His fingers found her magic button and she screamed her joy as she climaxed. She could feel the spasms of her body clenching his thick staff and he too cried out and poured his seed into her. Breathless, the two lovers collapsed on the cloth and lay entwined as their bodies calmed.

Later, calm and replete, they talked, about loving and beauty. "I understand," Doma said. "And it's all wonderful."

"Will you come here every night for a week and let me love you? You will learn, but I will not teach you. You will teach yourself as you did this night."

They met each night at the cove and loved and learned. As they walked toward the village on their last night together, F'am said, "I know how much you have learned, and I have learned from you."

"Will you tell the men of the village how talented I've become?"

"No," F'am said. "You will tell them, not with words, but with the confidence of a woman who knows how wonderful it can be in i'i."

"But I'm still plain. Can you make me beautiful?"

He turned her to face him in the moonlight. "You are beautiful as long as you believe it. Can you see your beauty reflected in my eyes?"

Doma looked and saw that, indeed she was beautiful. "Yes," she said softly. "I can see."

"Men who are worthy of you will be able to see it too." And with those words, F'am disappeared.

So Doma returned to the village. One afternoon, a man of twenty-two summers asked her to walk with him in the moonlight. "You are so beautiful," he said, as they walked toward the cove. He saw!

How the Gods Saved I'l

Excerpts from the field journals of Susan Talbot,
extraterrestrial ethnomythologist.

These field notes are a record of some of the amazingly diverse
tales I've learned in my years of travel. In order to understand
this story, you must know that the people of the planet Sh'a'i
are amazingly sexually active. There is no such thing as
monogamy and men and women engage in sexual play at
almost any time, with oral sex playing an important role in all
lovemaking. Why? This myth might explain it.

Long, long ago The People enjoyed lovemaking a great deal.
They played in the many waterfalls and pools of their island.
Children were many and The People prospered. Then some-

thing happened and the women suddenly wanted nothing to do with sex. They seemed to have forgotten how wonderful good lovemaking could be, viewing it as ugly and invasive. Soon the situation became so unpleasant that the men stopped trying to pleasure the women and rather than be denied, the men began to force the women to share i'i, as sexual relations were called. It became an ugly downward spiral, and eventually there was little i'i at all. No one received or gave any pleasure. The world was a sad place and there were few children. The People seemed to be destined to disappear from Sh'a'i.

The gods had tried to let The People solve their own problems but finally one day several of them looked down from the sacred mountain and saw a man forcing a woman to copulate with him. Some evil spirit had obviously placed some kind of spell on The People and it wasn't going to disappear. They knew they had to intervene.

Some of the gods discussed how to proceed and eventually it was decided that the god F'am, protector of the home and children, the lover of all women, would adopt human form and come to earth. He walked the land for many turns but wasn't able to discover why the women resisted so violently and why the men didn't try to woo them. For almost a season he sat with the women at the washing river, joined men in their hunting, sat with the mothers at their cooking fires, but couldn't find out what the source of the problem was. All that the women would say was that i'i was at best necessary to make children, and at worst a terrible invasion of their bodies. All the men knew was that when their body wanted i'i the only way to satisfy it was to copulate and that they would do it whether the women wanted it or not. In desperation, F'am took a particularly handsome human form and tried to seduce a few different women. Despite all his charm and seductive powers he had no luck. The women flatly refused his every effort.

One afternoon he encountered a particularly pleasing woman drawing water at the well. "Good afternoon," he said, giving her his best smile.

"Good afternoon to you, sir," she said. "Welcome."

"Thank you. I'm F'am."

Obviously not knowing who he was, the woman reached out and politely took his hand in greeting. "My name is T'ama'i."

They talked for a while and F'am was at his most appealing. He openly flirted with T'ama'i and, although she was charming and welcoming, she seemed unwilling to go any further than talk. Finally, F'am invited her to sup with him in a secluded glade in the forest and she accepted.

He arrived before she did and set out all the most alluring foods, especially those with aphrodisiac properties. When she arrived the cloth was spread with the finest delicacies. The trees around the glade sang in the afternoon breeze and the birds added their music to the setting. "This is a wonderful feast," she exclaimed. "Why have you gone to all this trouble?"

"It's no trouble. Here, sit and eat with me." Together they enjoyed the exotic foods. He fed her sweets and savories with his fingers. He dipped her finger in d'a, a honeylike substance, and sucked each digit into his mouth. To no avail. Every time he got close enough to touch her more, she backed away. "You are so beautiful and so desirable. You know I want you. Why won't you lie with me?" he asked.

"Is that what you want?" Angrily, she tried to stand but he pulled her back down.

"And why not? We like each other and we can while away the rest of this turn together."

"No. I'm sorry but no. You are very pleasing to the eye and you have an alluring way about you but I don't want to do that with anyone, even you. No. Absolutely no."

F'am decided that she obviously didn't know the joys of i'i so he held her hand tightly. "Let me show you how wonderful it can be."

"No. Let me go." She struggled, trying to pull her hand away from his strong grasp but she couldn't get free.

F'am thought about it for only a moment, then he made a rash decision. The glade was full of soft slender vines and he used the strongest to quickly tie her wrists together. He picked her up and carried her struggling body to a tree and fastened her hands to a branch several feet above her head. With her hands in the air, he quickly pulled the loose clothing from her body.

"You have a magnificent body," he crooned. "Your breasts are so full, your nipples tipped with copper. Your belly is rounded and your thighs smooth and white." He walked around behind her and slowly stroked her spine. "Your back is so soft, your skin like the finest garment."

T'ama'i squirmed, trying to free herself, but her hands were held fast. F'am slipped his fingers through her long hair, lifting it from her long white neck. He kissed her nape, then licked a path down the slender column. "So magnificent," he purred into her ear. "So easy to kiss."

"Please, sir," T'ama'i said, "I don't want you so close to me. I know what you're thinking and I don't want to. It's horrible."

"Why do you think so?"

"I don't think so, I know so. It's uncomfortable. It's awful and ugly." She started to cry.

F'am almost took pity on her, but he reasoned that maybe he could show her how wrong she was. "My precious," he purred, "making love is wonderful, if only you will give it a chance." He moved around her and combed his fingers through her hair, cupping the back of her head and staring into her eyes. "You're so wrong about loving. I'i is the most pleasurable, the most luscious, the most . . ." He slowly brought his lips to hers, licking and tasting every inch of her delectable mouth. He used all his skill to bring out a response but the more he tried, the more she tried to pull away.

As he pondered, he heard a distant laugh. He turned, gazing into the far distance. Again he heard the laugh. Then he knew. Sk'ala'i, the god of mischief and ill fortune had something to do with all of this. "Sk'ala'i," he said to the wind, "this is your doing. Why?"

"Why not?" a distant voice said. "I've enjoyed watching The People struggle. It amuses me."

"You cast a spell on them?"

"Only the women. I took away all of their arousing places and counted on the men's laziness to do the rest. You can see now that I was right. When the women resisted even a little the men stopped trying to seduce and just took." There was loud laughter. "It was fun to see how bad things got."

"Take the spell off," F'am cried.

The answer was only the sigh of the wind and a distant moan, then silence. Then a female voice whispered on the warm southern breeze. "I'm sorry I've been too involved in other things to see what was happening. Although I cannot undo Sk'ala'i's spell, I can cast one of my own. The People have never before engaged in oral sex, so Sk'ala'i didn't think to remove the pleasure from it. I've placed a magic button between every woman's legs and nothing Sk'ala'i can do can spoil it. Be patient and you'll know what to do."

"Thank you, A'wa, for your help." He looked at T'ama'i.

"Did you hear? Sk'ala'i cast a spell to take away all your pleasure places and make you think loving was horrible. I'i isn't bad or wrong or ugly. It's beautiful."

"I heard nothing but the wind," T'ama'i said, gazing into the distance.

F'am thought about the words only he had heard. A'wa's spell was the answer. A magic button. He lifted T'ama'i in his strong arms, placed her legs over his shoulders and supported her back against the trunk of the tree. Then he touched her between her legs, softly brushing her woman's folds. He smiled when he heard her sharp intake of breath as he touched a small bead of hard flesh.

"What are you doing?" she gasped.

"I am showing you pleasure," F'am said, sliding his fingers through her most intimate flesh, stroking the special spot. Then he lowered his lips and sucked her into his mouth, softly pulling and releasing this new center of her sex. He felt her shudder and, as he sucked, he slowly slid one finger into her channel.

"What are you doing?" T'ama'i asked, her breathing ragged and her heart pounding.

"A'wa gave you a special magic button that will show you the joy in i'i. I'm just helping you learn about it." For long minutes he sucked and used his finger to arouse her passion. It wasn't long before he felt her body begin to buck. The joy of her excitement almost overwhelmed him, but he kept licking.

When her breathing became more labored and he could feel her tremble he whispered, "Is this so bad?"

"Oh no," T'ama'i whispered. "It's wonderful. I've never felt like this before."

"Shall I stop now?" F'am asked, licking the length of her slit with the flat of his tongue. "You know where this is leading."

"Can you make i'i feel this good?" she asked.

"Better," F'am said. "But not yet." He continued playing with her magic button and as he did he slid a second finger to join the first inside T'ama'i's body. His body throbbed with the excitement of her and it became more and more difficult to go slowly. No, he told himself. Show her pleasure first. "Tell me how it feels," he begged.

"It's so good," she moaned. "Don't stop touching me."

F'am decided it was all right to let her down, so he untied her hands and laid her on the blanket where they had shared their meal. He crouched between her legs and stroked the insides of her thighs. "Would you like me to do more?"

"If it will feel that good, yes," T'ama'i said. "Please."

F'am smiled, then lowered his head and feasted on her now-wet body. He tasted her honey, licking and sucking, playing her like a fine instrument with his fingers and his mouth. Finally, when he was sure she could climb no higher, he undressed quickly and filled her waiting body with his erection. Over and over he thrust into her as she screamed with pleasure. Finally he emptied himself into her with a roar.

Later, he said, "It can be that wonderful with any man who knows the secret of your magic button. Would you like to love like that with other men?"

She looked a bit dazed, but said quickly, "Oh yes."

So over the next years, F'am taught the men of The People about this new magic and he taught the women how to learn about their bodies so they could help the men. Slowly, Sk'ala'i's spell wore off and both the men and the women enjoyed pleasing and taking pleasure in all ways. But the magic button became the center of their love play and the men became so skilled with their mouths that they could arouse a woman just by licking their lips.

Now there are statues to F'am and A'wa in almost every home. His image always has a large penis and an even larger smile. Her statue is always seated, with her hand between her thighs.

The Maid

Dear Reader,
This last story centeres on the Eros Hotel, a place where, for a hefty fee, any fantasy can be made real. Since I love this idea so much, don't be surprised if I write a novel based on these delicious activities. Enjoy. And let me know what you think of the idea of a novel. Drop me a line at Joan@JoanELloyd.com. —J.E.L.

The Eros hotel provided everything for its clients, but for the $1,000 per hour charge on his credit card, Brad expected this kind of service. He hurriedly changed into the clothes had been given, an outfit appropriate to his role, master of the nineteenth-century estate. He was impatient, but he understood the need for the trappings of his fantasy. He also enjoyed the anticipation. In his eagerness he almost didn't button the front of the vest. Finally he sighed and fastened his vest, then the jacket, dropping the large gold watch into the vest pocket, fob linked through the buttonhole.

He glanced in the full-length mirror in the dressing room, then slipped his twentieth-century clothing, wallet, and keys into the high-tech safe and set a new combination. Eros thought of even the smallest details. Everything complete, he walked through the door and down the hall to Room 12. Who would he find this time? He'd been to the Eros Hotel almost a dozen times and he'd yet to encounter the same woman twice.

He opened the door to Room 12 and strode inside. Walk like your character, he had read in the instructions months earlier, and you'll become him. "There's no one here to take my jacket," he called, unfastening the buttons he'd closed only moments earlier.

"I'm so sorry, sir," a soft, feminine voice with a slight British accent called from beyond another door. "I'm really sorry but I'll just be a moment. Please excuse me, sir."

Brad sighed. "Be quick about it," he called. "You know I don't like to be kept waiting. My servants should be prepared to see to my every need."

"Oh yes, sir," the voice said. He heard the door open then caught his first glimpse of his lady for the evening. She looked to be about twenty-five, tiny, probably no more than five feet tall, with her brown hair stuffed beneath a cloth cap. She was not really pretty, but desirable somehow, with large brown eyes and a thoroughly kissable lipstick-reddened mouth. She wore a traditional maid's uniform of white blouse and white apron, but her black skirt was short and fluffy. She also wore long mesh stockings and ridiculously high heels. Well maybe it wasn't a traditional uniform but rather the one he'd seen in several of his favorite porn movies.

"May I take your coat, sir?" she asked, her eyes downcast.

Brad stopped staring and snapped back into character, handing the "maid" his jacket. "You certainly may. What's your name?"

"Bridget," the girl said. "I'm new, just hired this week." There was a trace of an Irish lilt in her speech. "I hope you'll forgive my tardiness in welcoming you home."

"I'll consider it. Where's my coffee?"

Apparently flustered, the girl retreated into the other room, to return a few moments later with a cup and saucer balanced on a small tray, a silver coffee pot in her other hand. She placed the pot on the small table beside the "master's chair" and motioned for Brad to sit down. As he settled into the wing-back chair she poured him a cup of steaming coffee and said, "I'm told you like it black, sir."

Eros knew all his likes and dislikes, down to the tiniest detail. "That's right. Stand beside me and tell me why you were delayed in answering my summons."

Bridget stood beside Brad's chair, her thigh brushing his elbow. "I was fixing my stockings, sir," she said. "I had gotten a tear in one and had to change." She lifted one leg for his inspection. "See? It wouldn't do for me to appear in anything imperfect."

Brad glimpsed the ruffled garter just at the level of the short skirt, then reached out and touched the shapely leg beneath the rough mesh. "That's certain," he said, "but how did you manage to damage your first one? They cost money, you know."

Primly, Bridget gazed at the floor, her hands clasped in front of her. "I'm really sorry, sir. I was making up the bed in the next room and I caught my leg on an uneven spot on the frame. I'll pay for the stocking of course."

"Of course, but you'll have to pay for your clumsiness too." He touched the inside of her thigh and, as she stood beside him, slid his hand upwards. As he reached the garter, he felt her tremble, but he slipped his hand further up, over her smooth skin. Expecting to find the crotch of her panties, he was surprised when he touched her naked, wet pussy. He almost lost it right there, but instead slowly stroked her hot flesh and cupped her plump buttocks. "I won't dismiss you for your tardiness or your clumsiness but you'll have to be punished so you'll be sure it won't happen again. Do you understand?"

"Yes, sir," she whispered. Brad could feel her shiver and hear her breathing speed up. The Eros always fitted the women to their roles so he knew she'd get off on the same things that he wanted today. That was one of the most delicious things about Eros. The women always seemed to be enjoying things as much as he did. "Over my knee."

Bridget bent over, slowly settling across his lap. He knew she could feel the growing bulge in the front of his trousers, but he was well able to wait, and, of course, it was in the woman's best interest to go as long as she could. The cleverness of making the payment an hourly rate meant that the women wanted him to last, yet be completely satisfied so he'd return often. One of the women had told him that they receive additional compensation if the customer returns, even if it isn't for them specifically. Bridget wiggled as if getting comfortable across his thighs. Then he raised her skirt.

God, her ass was gorgeous, creamy white skin with a slight brown shadow in the crease between her thighs, the entire picture framed by her skirt and black hose. Slowly he swirled his palm over her skin, relishing the expectation, both hers and his. "You know that I'm doing this just to teach you a lesson, don't you?"

"Of course, sir. I know I must be suitably chastised."

"Right. I think ten ought to suffice. Count them for me."

"One," she whispered as his palm fell onto her ass-cheek.

"Louder," Brad snapped, slapping her other cheek, harder this time.

"Two!" she cried.

"Better." His hand fell a third time, then a fourth, each slap followed by Bridget's count. A fifth and sixth followed, then Brad stopped to savor the moment. Her cheeks were becoming bright pink, hot beneath his resting palm. "You have four more to go," he said, "but you can make it easy or difficult. Do you want to lessen your punishment, my dear?"

"Oh yes, sir. What must I do?"

Brad pushed her to the floor between his spread knees and unzipped his fly. He merely pointed to his hard cock thrusting from his trousers, glad that he never wore underwear during his visits to Eros. Shyly she gazed up at him from her position between his thighs. She licked her lips and smiled. "Oh yes, sir." She took his cock in her hand and moved her fingers so that he felt the need to come despite his best efforts. This was the best, using all his willpower to resist ejaculation. Eros knew that about him too. "Not so fast," he snapped.

"Sorry, sir," she said, a grin on her face. Then she lowered her reddened lips to the tip of his cock and slowly sucked the tip into her warm wet mouth. As she sucked she tightened her grip on the base of his erection so he couldn't come if he wanted to. The pressure was immense, but the pleasure was still better. God, she had a talented mouth, causing just the right amount of suction and swirling her tongue over the tip of his prick. He considered whether he wanted to come in her mouth or her pussy and decided that he wanted her beautiful little snatch around him when came. But that wouldn't be for quite a while.

"Enough," he said, his voice harsh. "You still have four slaps remaining."

"Yes, sir," she said, standing and then stretching out across his lap, her elbow pressing against his naked, wet cock, driving him mad with lust. Her ass-cheeks were still pink, but he reddened them considerably with his next two slaps. "You didn't count. That's five additional for your disobedience."

Genuine tears flowed down her face as she looked at him, "Please, sir, no more."

"Unfortunately it's your own fault. And I'll need the paddle to do these right."

"Oh, no, not the paddle." There was a gleam of pleasure in her eye as she rose, and fetched a wooden paddle from a drawer. He had known that all the implements he could want would be somewhere in the room. She knelt before him and presented him with the paddle, eyes downcast. He held it, stroking the smooth wood, as Bridget again lay across his lap. He caressed her ass with the cool surface, making circles over her fiery flesh.

"You're making it worse," Bridget whimpered, "making me wait, sir."

"I know," Brad said, smiling. Then he raised the paddle and slapped it smartly on her butt. "Six," she said.

"Actually it's seven but we'll accept your count." He delivered the remaining smacks over the sounds of her crying, then he urged her to a standing position in front of him. "Get some lotion and I'll soothe your bum."

From the same drawer from which she had gotten the paddle she pulled a tube and handed it to him. Then she turned around and knelt on the carpet so he could get a perfect view of her flaming ass. He squeezed a large dollop of the lotion onto his palm, then slowly rubbed it over her skin.

"All right, stand up." She stood before him, trembling. "Make me ready." She rubbed her hands over her buns then slid her slippery fingers up and down over his cock. Then she quickly opened a packet and unrolled a condom over his throbbing cock.

Rising, she grinned at him, then slipped back into character, her eyes looking downward. Brad placed one hand behind each of her knees and pulled her forward so she was kneeling on the chair, her pussy poised over his cock. "Down!" She lowered her body until he could slide his erection over her hot, slippery ass-cheeks. God, he loved the feel of a heated ass against his thighs. She wiggled, allowing her body to inflame him. Slowly she allowed his rock-hard prick to penetrate her. She felt just right, so tight around him. Her hot cheeks against his groin, her hands on his shoulders, the sight of her fully dressed, her head thrown back in ecstasy all conspired to take his control. His orgasm burst from him as he drove his cock deep into her, thrusting over and over. He couldn't catch his breath or prevent the loud scream that erupted from the depths of his soul. It had never been any better.

Bridget collapsed against his cloth-covered chest, panting

as hard as he was. "I'm not supposed to slip out of character," she said, "but that was fabulous . . ." she winked, ". . . sir."

Eros. It was as it had always been, a totally unqualified success. He'd be back, whether to Room 12 or to another, he'd be back. Soon.

Dear Reader,

I know you enjoyed reading the stories in Naughty Bedtime Stories *as much as I enjoyed writing them, and Ed enjoyed editing them. They led to some great lovemaking for us, and, I hope, for you as well.*

Drop me a note at Joan@JoanELloyd.com and let me know which tales were your special favorites. And if you have any ideas for stories I should write, let me know. You might also want to visit my website at JoanELloyd.com. I write and post a new short story each month and, in addition, you'll find information about all my books, forums filled with sexual advice and information, and lots more.

You can look forward to many more delicious tales and more great sex.

—J.E.L.